‖‖‖ ‖ ‖‖‖‖‖ ‖ ‖‖‖ ‖‖‖‖‖‖ ‖‖
I0689744

THE DANGER TRAIL

Also by Lee Martin

Shadow on the Mesa
Fast Ride to Boot Hill
The Last Wild Ride
The Grant Conspiracy: Wake of the Civil War
Fury at Cross Creek
In Mysterious Ways
Revenge at Rawhide
The Maverick Gun
Fury at Sweetwater Pass
The Lone Rider
Black River
Dead Man's Trail
Valley of the Lawless
Track the Men Down

The Darringer Brothers Series:
Trail of the Fast Gun
Trail of the Long Riders
Trail of the Hunter
Trail of the Circle Star
Trail of the Restless Gun
Trail of the Dangerous Gun

and coming soon…
Hang Town

THE DANGER TRAIL

LEE MARTIN

VACA MOUNTAIN PRESS
VACAVILLE, CALIFORNIA, USA

Copyright © 1994, 2020 by Lee Martin

ALL RIGHTS RESERVED. In accordance with the U.S. Copyright Act of 1976, no part of this publication may be reproduced, distributed, or transmitted in any form or by any means, or stored in a database or retrieval system, without prior written permission of the author.

This book is a work of fiction. All names, characters, places and events are products of the author's imagination or are used fictitiously, and any resemblance to actual persons, living or dead, or to actual places or businesses, is entirely coincidental.

Vaca Mountain Press
Large Print Paperback ISBN 13: 978-1-952380-46-4

Also available in
Paperback ISBN 13: 978-1-952380-44-0
Kindle ISBN 13: 978-1-952380-45-7

Library of Congress Catalog Card Number: 94-94251

Interior design by Eddie Vincent, ENC Graphic Services
Cover design by Christopher Wait for ENC Graphic Services
Cover images © Getty Images

Published by Vaca Mountain Press

Visit Lee Martin Westerns on Facebook.

To all of my wonderful family,
and in the fond memory of
my beloved mother,
my beautiful sister Arlene,
our rough riding brothers,
and for Jim Liontas.

THE DANGER TRAIL

ONE

Even in his heavy coat, Bronco Wade felt the chill of night as he squatted with his plate of beans by the blazing fire. "Me and Curly been followin' your herd for some time, Biscuits. Whose outfit is this, anyhow?"

Scraping off the backboard of the chuck wagon, the elderly cook yawned. "We're the last of several drives they sent up from Texas. Already brought up one of the best herds of horseflesh you ever saw. Gonna be the biggest spread in Montana Territory. The Trigger Bar. Belongs to Frank Sladek and his sons."

Bronco swallowed hard, his skin suddenly crawling. Curly choked on his coffee and spit it out, his face as red as his wiry beard. The two men were frozen. Bronco, a husky man who was half Curly's sixty years, stared down at his white knuckles as he gripped the hardtack and tin plate.

Biscuits didn't seem to notice as he wiped his fingers on his apron. "The other campfire, that covered wagon over there by that big cottonwood. Miss Charity Sladek and her chaperone."

Bronco stiffened and saw Curly's weathered face breaking into a sudden, hot sweat. Both felt like peeling off their heavy wool coats and checking their six-guns. Bronco pushed his wide-brimmed Stetson back from his damp brow. The cook continued to chatter as he cleaned off the chuck wagon.

"Storm comin' up fast, and it's mighty cold. Sky's black as the ace of spades. I know this country. Thunder can be so loud you think it's in your pocket. Ain't had a stampede since Colorado, but we're plenty worried right now. Got around fifteen hundred out there."

Bronco glanced at the shaken Curly and asked the questions for his silent partner."I heard of the Sladeks, Didn't know there was a daughter."

"Well, she was a foundling left at some church down in Texas. Frank was a widower but hired a woman to look after her. He got to be her legal guardian. When she was ten, Frank sent her back east to school with his cousin's widow. That was fifteen years ago. Frank got married again last year and sent his sister to get Miss Charity. We met them both in Cheyenne off the train."

Bronco was grim. "Woman's got no place on a trail drive. Who's headin' it up?"

"Fellow named Hooper from Sladek's Texas spread. Him and five others. We lost Sladek's Montana foreman some time back. Hooper said his horse rolled over on 'im. Buried him back along Crazy Woman Creek. Seven others took off for the goldfields. The only Montana hands left are the Tyree brothers. The young one's been workin' as a wrangler."

"You're shorthanded," Bronco said.

"Not to hear Hooper tell it. I tell you boys, I ain't too happy we turned north from the Bozeman. Hooper claimed there'd be better grass up here, even though the Tyrees warned him it's only been two years since Custer got killed in '76, and them Injuns are still hoppin' mad."

"Why'd the Sladeks move up from Texas?"

"Free grass. But they'll be runnin' roughshod over everyone up here, just like in Texas, and you can bet on it. I sure wouldn't want to get in their way."

"This Sladek, does he have sons?"

"Used to have five. Three of 'em got killed by a gang of outlaws in Texas about fifteen years ago. Feller named Jim Hodges and a dozen killers."

Bronco's face went hot. "How'd they know who done it?"

"One of the sons was still alive when Hooper and his men came along, and he lived long enough to say how they'd been hangin' a rustler when this Hodges and his gang came shootin'. The rustler got away. Fellow named Wiley Haines."

Bucket in hand, the cook turned and headed across the open land toward the far creek and the cottonwoods. Curly and Bronco sat staring at each other and the distant wagon with its small flickering campfire. It was a cold spring night with black clouds hovering, and they were in a lot of trouble.

They could hear the cattle bellowing in the distance, but there were no other night sounds except the crackle of the fire.

Bronco was sitting with his elbows on his crossed knees, sipping his coffee. His nose, broken twice, was slightly crooked in a weathered face with rough features and ice blue eyes. Both feet had been stomped on and his left leg had been cracked more than once.

Curly hunched up as he drew his blankets around him, his green eyes glistening wet and voice low. "We been avoidin' them Sladeks for fifteen years. They find out I'm Haines and you're Hodges, we're deader'n last year's cowchip."

Bronco spoke in a whisper. "Is Charity your daughter?"

Curly slowly rubbed his wet face with the back of his hand. "Seems like. That was her ma's name. And that tells me Sladek sure enough knew who she was."

Bronco drew his heavy coat more closely over his leather vest and soiled blue shirt. His britches were stiff from mud and too many river crossings. Weary, he looked toward the other campfire and the Sladek wagon, but there was no sign of the women.

Bronco grimaced, shaking his head. "Jim Hodges, outlaw."

"No Sladek's gonna admit a fifteen-year-old kid wasted three of their own. But they figure out who we are, they won't waste no time makin' us dead. We get out of here afore daylight tomorrow."

"I was a skinny kid half my size. And my nose has been busted twice. They'd never recognize me. And you growed that beard and lost most of your hair."

"I ain't takin' no chances."

Bronco drew his blankets around him and leaned back on his saddle. He pulled his Stetson down on his lined brow and stretched. "Before we leave, don't you figure your daughter oughta know she wasn't thrown away?"

"And tie her down to an ugly, broken old cowhand who ain't got nothin' 'cept what he carries on his saddle? She was only two when I left her in the church sound asleep. She probably hates me for leavin' her. Besides, who'd believe a fella like me was her pa?"

"You know blamed well you want to see her."

Curly's voice turned to a whisper. "I don't want her to see me." He turned his face away and pulled his hat over his eyes to hide his face.

And Bronco lay with his eyes closed, thinking back all those years to his own father. The terrible image of Rad Hodges dangling from a cottonwood was always there, and the pain and suffering of a fourteen-year-old boy would never leave him. Curly had nearly died the same way a year later, and Bronco never wanted to see that again.

They were disturbed as a rider approached, and they both sat up to watch a tall, husky man with near-white eyes and a scar across his left cheek. Wearing a heavy coat, he had a flat nose and looked mighty unfriendly as he dismounted and walked over for a meal.

He paused, glaring down at them. "Who the devil are you?"

The cook came back with a bucket of water and paused. "Lazlo, these are friends of mine. So just eat."

"Yeah, well, I don't like grub riders."

Bronco leaned back on his saddle and grinned as he pushed his hat from his brow. "You always this friendly?"

"We got our hands full, and we ain't got time to feed no saddle tramps. Both of you, move out afore daylight, or I'll kick you out."

"One of these days, I'll teach you some manners," Bronco said, "but I'm too sleepy for the likes of you."

Lazlo snickered and turned to take a plate from the cook, eating while standing and glaring at the visitors. Bronco pulled his hat down and pretended to sleep, as did Curly, neither of them moving until Lazlo was riding back to the herd.

"That was close," the cook said. "He's near killed a couple men with his bare hands. Used to fight for money."

Curly yawned and stretched. "Bronco can take 'im."

Bronco chuckled. "Yeah, sure."

It was colder by the minute, and the two friends curled up in their blankets. Both men had troubled memories. Curly was having a difficult time sleeping because he knew that a few hundred yards away was his daughter, and there was nothing he could do about it, but he was as weary as Bronco.

Exhaustion, the distant call of a lone coyote, and the crackling fire were lulling them toward sleep when the black sky rumbled. And so did the ground, trembling as the cattle darted about on the hills north of camp, fighting the control of the herders.

Lightning streaked across the sky like the crack of a whip. Curly and Bronco were already wearing slickers and saddling up. The remuda of around thirty horses was roped off in the trees, and every horse there was dancing around.

"We're in for it," Curly said.

The ground was shaking under their boots as they sprang astride and headed for the herd at a lope, but they were too late.

Under the rapid flashes of lightning that crackled across the black sky, the herd was already breaking out. The riders were circling, shouting and waving, but a loud roll of thunder set the herd into a run; they spilled forth toward the west, horns clanging.

Two riders were racing for the lead, heads down, whipping their mounts frantically. They were on the south side of the herd.

Suddenly, there was another crack of lightning, splitting the ground in front of the cattle. They spun south, right into the two riders, crashing over one who went down with his horse while the other frantically tried to turn back for his friend, then turned his horse and raced to outrun them.

Curly and Bronco headed for him, firing their weapons.

The rider's horse stumbled and fell, rolling across the cowboy and away. The cowboy staggered up from the ground, dazed. Bronco swept by and seized him by the belt, whipping him up across his pommel, whirling his buckskin about as the cattle bumped the gelding in all directions, shoving it crazily forward.

"My brother!" the youth shouted as he tried to get upright.

Curly had pulled aside in a desperate bid for safety. Bronco was praying his buckskin could outrun the cattle with two men on board, and he dug in his heels. The gelding sprang forward, leaping brush and rocks as lightning flashed in front of them. The herd spun away and back toward the west, and Curly was back at Bronco's side.

The young, red-faced cowboy, yellow hair near white in the flashes of lightning, was trying to twist around on the pommel. Bronco let him slide down to the ground, then gave him a hand up to sit behind him as he reined his buckskin about.

The cowboy was frantic. "I'm Tom Tyree. That was my brother Billy who went down."

The herd was circling up to the west, and Bronco rode slowly toward the fallen youth, who was curled up against the belly of his horse between its legs. Tom jumped down and ran to kneel by his brother, his hand on the cold face under the crushed hat.

"God, Billy," he murmured. "I never got to say I loved yuh."

Tears were on his cheeks as he hesitated to lift Billy's hat, fearful of what horror he would see. Bronco knelt, choking on his own emotions, putting a firm hand on Tom's shoulder.

Tom was wiping the tears as fast as they came. "He was a good brother. A bothersome kid, but real smart. Drove me crazy sometimes, but now what am I gonna do? He was all I had, and now he's gone."

Bronco squeezed Tom's shoulder, for he was remembering how it had been when his own father had died, leaving him alone at fourteen. He was feeling the pain all over again.

Tom sniffed. "All he ever wanted from me was my black swimmin' horse and my new Stetson. I'd give 'em to 'im tomorrow, if I could just have Billy—"

It was then that Billy looked up from under his hat.

"Lord almighty," gasped Tom. "You ain't dead."

"You ain't got my fancy saddle yet."

"Are you hurt?"

"Of course I'm hurt, dad blame it. Got kicked in the head a dozen times. Look what they did to my hat. And I was stepped on all over the place."

"Can you move?"

"Not a chance."

Bronco, amazed, sat back on his heels.

But Tom was turning red. "You let me sit here blubberin' over you all this time? I oughta whup you good."

Billy's round pink face was gaining color, and he grinned, showing some crooked teeth. "I'll take your swimmin' horse though. And that new hat."

"No deal. You was trickin' me."

"First time you ever said anything good about me."

"And the last, dad bum it. But right now, we've got to rig somethin' to get you out of here in case them cattle head back this way."

Curly came to help. They brought limbs from the cottonwoods at the creek and made a quick travois with saddle blanket and slicker, then tied Billy down on it and covered him with another slicker.

With Tom running along at his brother's side, Curly trailed the contraption from his bay. The broken cowboy bounced along as best he could, swearing loudly. Rain began to fall, soft at first, then heavy and persistent.

Back at the camp, Curly and Bronco dismounted to help Tom get his brother under the tarp the cook had suspended on poles some ten feet out from the chuck wagon, covering the campfire. Billy was in his late teens and Tom in his early twenties. They had round faces with pale blue eyes and wide mouths. Biscuits was working on Billy.

"Your left arm's broke, son. I got to set it."

As lightning flashed again on the far horizon, Curly and Bronco mounted and rode back toward the herd to be sure it was contained. Every time the light streaked across the sky, the cattle broke free.

They met up with a burly cowhand who was shouting at them. "We got to circle 'em."

And try they did. The lightning disappeared as the heavy rain beat on them like bullets. The other riders came into view in the dark, and between the six of them and Curly and Bronco, they were able to contain the herd until it milled in a great, restless, moving circle.

They saw Lazlo glaring at them as he passed.

The lack of lightning and the fierceness of the heavy rain seemed to allow calm, temporarily. But the burly cowhand twisted about in the saddle, rain pouring off his hat and down his slicker. He had a rough face and a handlebar mustache, and he was still worried.

"If we don't get no thunder, we may be all right. My name's Krinkle, boys. Did the Tyrees go down?"

"They're all right," Curly said.

"Glad of it. They're good hands."

"You're from the Sladek Texas spread?" Bronco asked.

"No, these other fellows are. Me, I hired on for the drive."

They paused, hunched up in the rain as an ugly man with a large nose rode up to them, his voice gravelly. "I'm Hooper, the trail boss. Where'd you fellas come from?"

"We were just sharin' your camp," Bronco said.

Instead of thanking them, the ugly man rode past them and around the herd. Krinkle pulled his hat down tight and adjusted his slicker.

"Well, we're much obliged. Who are you anyway?"

"Curly Watson, and that's Bronco Wade."

"Bronco Wade? Weren't you breakin' horses for the cavalry?"

Curly nodded and bragged some, but Bronco

14

drew his slicker more tightly about him. He was thinking about what would happen if any of these men recognized them.

Bronco and Curly hunched over in the cold rain and headed back.

The cook and the Tyree brothers were under the tarp by the campfire. Billy was lying in some blankets, his left arm in a crude cast of lime and tightly bound cloth. Tom was sitting beside him, holding a cup of coffee in both hands.

Kneeling in front of them was a young woman in a dark blue cape, hood down from a head of gorgeous dark red hair that spilled about her face and throat.

Curly reined up. "She's there."

Bronco reached over and swatted the rump of Curly's mount, and they rode forward, dismounting near the camp. They loosened the cinches and tethered their horses, then returned to move under the tarp. It was a little crowded, and the rain was bowing the top of the canvas, but it was dry by the fire.

Curly could hardly walk, and Bronco had to pull him down to a sitting position as they both stared at the young woman.

Firelight danced in her hair, and long thick lashes flickered over blue-green eyes. She had a

15

slim nose that tilted up slightly, full lips, and a tiny white scar on her chin. She was incredibly beautiful, taking Bronco's breath away.

Curly had no color in his face as he gazed at her.

"That's him," Torn said, nodding toward Bronco. "He picked me right out of the stampede."

"I'm Charity Sladek. And I thank you."

"That's Curly Watson, ma'am. I'm Bronco Wade."

"The real Bronco Wade?" Billy asked, looking up.

Bronco shrugged and nodded. This time Curly didn't do any bragging. He was tongue-tied, staring at his daughter with his heart thumping away.

Billy was grinning at Bronco. "We heard about you when we was comin' through Wyomin' Territory. The Army hires you sometimes. And you rode Black Bottom over at Cheyenne last Fourth of July, a real bad one they said. And they say you ain't never been throwed."

Bronco felt uneasy. "Well, not by any horse I ever tried to break. But my buckskin's got a habit of surprisin' me and throwin' me off anytime he takes a mind."

Tom thought that was funny, but he was impressed.

"You ain't got a big head. Our pa would have liked you, bless his soul. You got family, Bronco?"

"No."

The cook poured coffee for Bronco and the shaken Curly, but he frowned at Charity. "You ain't supposed to be around the men without Mrs. Paulson. Frank Sladek will have my hide."

"Now don't scold me. Mrs. Paulson's asleep, and I was worried when I saw them bring Billy into camp."

Bronco felt awkward as he sat on his heels, coffee in hand, watching her as she turned to look at him. He felt his face grow hot as she spoke.

"You were brave to risk your life to save Billy."

"He'd have done it for me," Bronco said uneasily. "You're certainly modest for a Texan."

"How do you know we're from Texas?" Curly asked.

"By the wide brims on your hats and the way they're crimped up on top," she said with a smile. "I was only ten when I left Texas, but I remember a lot, I promise you."

Curly winced, looking away.

"And you don't have much of a drawl," she added, "but I can tell. And the way you both walk. With a swagger. Texans always got that way of walking like they own the country."

Bronco grinned but didn't respond.

She smiled and stood up slowly, the light caressing her face. Then she pulled the hood about her head, still smiling as she turned and went into the rain, heading, back to her wagon.

Curly, tongue-tied again, spun his hat on his fingers.

The cook built up the fire to keep the beans and coffee hot, then curled up under the wagon, and Billy went to sleep. Soon both were snoring gently.

Tom Tyree set his cup down and stood up. "If anything had happened to my brother, I don't know what I would have done. So thanks, Bronco."

Bronco nodded, and Tom secured another horse from the remuda and went back to the herd. Curly and Bronco were silent a long while as they huddled under the tarp and watched the rain beating the sod. They glanced at Billy and the cook, who were both sleeping soundly.

"What are we gonna do now?" Curly asked softly.

"I figure the best we can do is make sure she's safe afore we head out."

As they talked quietly by the fire, the herd was milling in the distance with Tom on his way to join it. Hooper rode alongside one of his men, a scrawny man with big eyes. He gazed up at the black, moving clouds in the rain, which was lighter now.

"Got a glimpse of the moon," Hooper said. "If things go right, it's gonna break up, Boney. And that means thunder."

"They'll be off again."

"We get another shot at 'em."

"You sure you want to go against Frank Sladek on this?"

"I ain't scared of him," Hooper growled. "And I'm tired of gettin' forty a month for all I done for him. We all risked our necks for him one time or another, and we got nothin' to show for it."

"Well, we're all gonna hang if we get caught."

"This time make sure the herd heads for the camp."

"The women too?"

"All of 'em. We don't want no witnesses."

TWO

Charity squirmed in her blankets, bumping against Nora Paulson. The wagon wasn't that wide, and it was filled with belongings, shoving the women into a slot in the center with Charity toward the rear. The tarp cover was whipping up and down in the wind as moonlight brushed through the clouds and brought a glow to the inside of the wagon.

"Charity, will you lie still?" the woman grumbled.

"I can't sleep. Poor Billy nearly died."

"Billy is a wrangler. A cowboy. Your father does not want you around them."

"He's not my father."

They both turned to face each other in the pale light as the hefty woman spoke harshly. "Charity, my brother brought you up as his

20

ward. He's your legal guardian. It's the same thing."

"No, it's not. That's why I call him Uncle Frank."

"Well, your own folks didn't want you, but he did, so you'd best be a little grateful."

"I am grateful," Charity said. "I came to Texas to see him several times, didn't I?"

"Well, you'd best not tell him where his money went. If he had known that our cousin's widow was keeping every penny and just tutoring you herself instead of sending you to that fancy school, he would have gone through the roof. And he might even have got her sent to jail for embezzlement."

"But you've promised not to tell him."

"No need, unless you give us trouble."

"I told you I'd do anything Uncle Frank wants. Just leave Miss Freddie alone. Besides, she earned the money and taught me well."

"Taught you well? You were nothing but a tomboy, out there herding her awful sheep and cows, riding bareback like some Indian. I saw you myself, all dirty and wearing men's britches. I'm sure glad Frank didn't see you," said Nora.

Charity smiled. "He would have a fit, wouldn't he?"

"It's not funny. That's why I dressed you up like a lady. He's got two sons left, Leo and Lucas, and you'll be marrying one of them. They want their women soft, but they're hard men, Charity. My husband was a weak man and died on the Texas border. But he wasn't a Sladek. And that's the kind of men it takes out here."

Charity snuggled deep in her blankets. "But Uncle Frank's remarried, and his new wife has a daughter my age. Maybe they've softened him up."

"Not Frank."

The moon disappeared behind moving clouds, and there was a dead silence as Mrs. Paulson turned back into her blankets.

Charity huddled in her bedding, but she was still cold.

Suddenly, a clap of thunder exploded above and again rumbled and rolled across the sky, so loud it burst into the wagon like a hammer, a roar that jolted them down with a blow. They were left momentarily deaf as they sat up in terror in the blackness. Again it rolled, shaking the wagon as if grizzlies had hold of the wheels.

"My God," Charity breathed.

Nora fumbled for the lantern, and the thunder struck again, hurting their ears and leaving them shaken as it rolled through like a tornado.

As Nora struck the match and the flickering light filled the smoked-glass chimney of the lamp, the wagon began to quiver and rock, the tarp caving in up front. The ground was shaking as cattle swarmed around them in panic.

And as their hearing returned, they heard thunder of the herd racing around them. They crawled in their nightclothes to the back of the wagon, trying to get out. Nora shoved Charity aside and climbed over the tailgate.

Charity grabbed her own blankets and tried to follow, but just then, a terrible force of terrified cattle hit the wagon, shoving the right wheels into the air; Charity cried out and was thrown backward.

The wagon bed went crazily into the air, taking her with it and coming down on top of her with a thud, crushing her with belongings and bedding. Pounding hoofs went around and over, thumping the boards and tarp in a furious stampede.

The sky rolled with thunder, again and again.

Frantic, fearful the wagon bed would crumble on top of her, Charity crawled to the edge. Nora Paulson's body lay just outside the wagon in the passing moonlight. But there were only a few steers on that side at the moment. If only she could make it to the big pine tree.

She could hear more cattle behind her, charging south across the camp, horns clanging. She dragged herself over the tailgate and dropped to the wet ground just as the wagon was smashed flat right next to her. A big steer bumped her as it passed, knocking her aside and down to her knees in the mud.

She looked up to see more cattle heading for her. She thought she could never escape, and her heart stopped as she turned to try to get some shelter from the wagon, until she heard a shout.

"Grab my hand."

It was Bronco, leaning from the saddle.

Clad only in a white nightgown of heavy cotton, Charity staggered to her bare feet and seized his left arm with her right hand. He jerked her up behind him, then spun his buckskin as the cattle crashed into his horse's rump. Charity clasped her hands in front of him and buried her face in his back.

Bronco rode with the tide and headed south, working his way west toward the creek and the grove of cottonwoods. Before they could clear the camp, the rest of the herd came rushing in, frantic, horns tossing, darting right and left, the leaders being pushed faster and faster by the rest.

Bronco's buckskin shot past the chuck wagon even as the cattle struck it down. They reached the creek and set their horses into a jump across it. The cook and Billy were with Curly in the rocks up the slope past the cottonwoods. The herd was heading south with Tom and the other riders trailing.

Thunder rolled again, but lightning flashed to the south, cutting right across the land like a torch. The cattle spun, rushing into themselves in terror as they turned back on the riders, who scattered, frantically firing their weapons into the air.

Watching the turmoil, Charity was numb as Bronco lowered her into Curly's waiting arms. She stumbled against Curly, who was clumsily trying to put a wool coat about her. She was barefoot, wet, and shivering, and she hugged him.

My little girl, Curly thought, tears in his eyes.

Thunder boomed like a blast of dynamite, hitting the clouds and the earth with a deafening roar. The horses jumped as the cook mumbled his prayers.

Charity was quivering all over, and Curly put a slicker over her coat and around her. She smiled at him, unaware of his inner turmoil and joy at being close to her. She sat down next to Billy, who was rolled up in his blankets.

With the cattle gone, Bronco returned to the broken wagon to retrieve some of Charity's clothes while the cook and Curly uprighted the overturned chuck wagon.

A fire was built against the rocks as first light crossed the land. The sky had cleared except for a few scattered clouds and a brilliant rainbow to the east.

Charity used the huge slicker she was wearing like a tent, and she managed to dry herself and pull on a riding skirt and boots, along with a blue velvet jacket over a white blouse, all underneath the slicker.

There was no sign of the cattle, but most of the remuda had wandered back. After Curly and Bronco buried Mrs. Paulson near where she had fallen, they helped Charity recover a carpetbag of her clothes from the fallen wagon. The cook managed a hot breakfast of bacon and beans, along with fresh coffee.

"Those hands out there are gonna need help,"

Curly said, downing his coffee. "We better get out there."

While they rounded up their horses, young Tom was out on the flats trying to circle some of the stray cattle.

Hooper was sitting on his weary horse on a knoll; Boney and Lazlo rode up to join him in the chilling rain that was falling hard and bitter.

"Them cattle are scattered from here to Sunday," Boney said, pulling his hat down tight.

"And all that money waitin' in Virginia City with all them hungry miners," Lazlo growled.

"Yeah," Boney said, "but here comes Tom."

Tom Tyree rode up onto them in the early light of day as the rain dribbled off their hat brims.

"They sure are scattered," Tom said resignedly.

Hooper leaned on his horn. "Yeah, well, how's everyone at camp?"

"Mrs. Paulson was killed. The others are okay."

Hooper grunted. "Well, it's gonna take days to run 'em down."

Tom studied the ugly man for a long moment, but Hooper was trail boss, and Tom shrugged. "We're already late gettin' here, but it's only a week to the Trigger Bar."

Hooper was startled. "A week?"

"Sure. You took a shortcut north through Injun country, remember? Saved a lot of time."

"Well, ain't that somethin'," Hooper said grimly.

Tom turned his horse and rode back down the slope, heading toward camp. Hooper and Boney stared after him, making faces. Lazlo shook his head.

"Yeah," Boney said. "Ain't that somethin'. We head out here so we can take over. Now we're too blamed close. Sladek could have scouts lookin' for us."

Hooper nodded. "And we got live witnesses."

"So what are we gonna do?"

"Bide our time. Wherever there's cows and money, there's a way to get some of it."

While Hooper and his five men set about tracking the herd with Tom assisting, Bronco and Curly rode out to join the hunt. After the two men had rounded up some fifty head from a far ravine, they reined up to rest their horses.

"I tell you, Bronco, she's the spittin' image of my wife. I'm so proud I could bust."

Bronco leaned on the pommel. "Well, you've got to know, the sooner we get out of here, the better."

It was then that Tom came riding over to

them. "Hooper was sure surprised when I told 'im we were a week from Bear Creek and the Trigger Bar."

"Maybe he won't try nothin' now," Curly said.

"Maybe he already did," Tom replied. "That stampede didn't have to head back toward camp. It sure looked like them cattle was gettin' some help turnin' south. I can't prove nothin', but I'd sure appreciate you fellas stickin' around."

"We'll stick awhile," Bronco said.

"Once we get to the main trail where the stage road is, it's a day north to the town and another day north from there to the ranch. No tellin' when the Sioux or Cheyenne will show up afore then. They raid the Crows off and on."

Tom rode back toward the milling cattle. Curly and Bronco sat in their saddles in silence for a while, gazing at the surrounding hills and busy creeks, the dark forests to the north, and the brilliant blue of the sky.

"What do you think?" Bronco asked.

"Well," Curly said, "when the storm hit, the Indians took shelter just like the rest of us. But now they'll be hungry, lookin' for game. Be some mule deer around, probably in velvet already. Elk maybe. Jackrabbits."

"Maybe they all went to Canada with Sittin' Bull," Bronco suggested.

"Seems like somethin' keeps happenin' to hold us here. Makes you wonder if the Good Lord don't have some thin' in mind."

But hours later, as they rested their weary horses on a knoll, a lazy buzzard sailing above on the wind, the two men stared off to the north horizon where some twenty horses and near-naked riders were quietly watching from a ridge.

"Sioux?" Bronco asked.

"Blamed if they don't look like Arapaho, and they're the meanest. But I ain't sure."

THREE

B ronco grimaced. "What now?"
"Keep ridin' like you don't see 'em."
"One of us better keep the camp in sight at all times."
Curly nodded. "It's the horses they'll be after, but they won't care who gets in the way."
"I got me a bad feelin'."
"Me too. We oughta be outta here and somethin' keeps happening to trap us. We're in quicksand, all right."
Abruptly, the Indians disappeared from sight. Curly passed the word to Hooper and his men, who were all skeptical, especially the snickering Lazlo.
Curly and Bronco kept hunting cattle and bringing them through the hollows toward the main herd. In midafternoon, they rested their

horses on a knoll, gazing at the herd already growing fast. But then they looked toward camp in surprise.

Riding toward them on a sorrel was Charity, wearing a man's battered hat with chinstrap and sitting the saddle astride. In place of her velvet jacket, she had donned Billy's wool coat. The sorrel loped easily with Charity riding like any cowhand, a lariat over the saddle horn. She reined up beside Curly. Her face was flushed from the chill and excitement of action.

"I came to help."

"You're a woman," Bronco said.

She smiled. "You noticed."

"Look," Curly said, "them cattle may be wore out, but everyone of 'em's plenty ornery. They'll knock you plumb out of the saddle."

"I know what I'm doing."

"You growed up in finishing school," Curly argued.

Bronco nodded. "This is man's work."

She lifted the lariat and built a loop. "Want to bet?"

"Listen," Curly said, anger rising. "You do as you're told and get back to camp."

"You can't tell me what to do," she said.

"I'm tellin' you. Get back to camp. I don't want you gored by some ornery cow. Or dallying off some of those pretty fingers."

"You have nothing to say about it," she said with a sweet smile.

Curly was half-rising out of his saddle. "Blast you, girl. If you don't get back to camp, I'm goin' to tan your hide. Now go on."

Charity giggled and dug in her heels, heading at a trot down the slope to where Tom was bringing another twenty head out of a draw. Loop swinging at her side, she helped turn the cattle like an old cowhand.

The two men watched from the hill, leaning on the pommels of their saddles and shaking their heads.

Bronco chuckled. "Well, you blew that one."

"Yeah, but look at her. She didn't learn that in no fancy school. She rides like a Comanche."

"Rides better'n you."

Curly grunted. "I sure was actin' like a father."

"Sounded that way to me."

They rode down to join Tom and Charity, and they had to admire her skill with a rope as well as the way she sat in the saddle, even when a cow charged and her horse reared. She spun it about and circled the cow once more, taking charge.

Curly could only shake his head.

While they worked to round up the cattle as the days drew long and Hooper kept his distance from Bronco and Curly, the Sladeks were busy working to build their ranch into a showplace. The outbuildings and vast array of corrals were spread on the flat and the grand new house on a knoll.

Frank and his wife of one year, Elva, were inside the two-story house. It was sparsely furnished, but it had plush drapes on large windows, a spiral staircase, and a plush green rug. The walls had fine paintings of Indians and the Oregon Trail.

Frank was at his desk near the fireplace, locking a large tin box and shoving the key inside his black leather vest.

Elva was hefty but handsome with a round face and gray-brown hair done up in tight curls, her dark eyes flashing. She was wearing a blue silk gown with velvet, trim and was carrying a decorated fan in her white fingers.

"Frank, we've just got to have a rosewood piano."

"You'll have anything you want, Elva. All I want is for Charity to marry one of my boys.

You take care of that."

"Don't forget my daughter Emmy Lou."

Frank, a big, good-looking man in his late fifties with harsh features, pulled his weathered hat down tight. He was wearing ranch clothes and smelled of sweat.

"I got two sons, and I want a lot of grandsons, so you just get busy with the arrangements."

She came to put her soft fingers at his face. "Frank, we have to remember propriety. And we must find a housekeeper soon. My hands are getting so rough and red. Remember how you like them soft and white."

She kissed his cheek, and he grunted as he went outside into the sunlight. She folded her arms and frowned, then turned to see her daughter coming down the stairs in a yellow dress, her brown hair done up in big curls. She was a pretty, slim girl with light brown eyes and slightly pointed chin.

"Emmy Lou, that's one of your prettiest gowns."

"I just felt like wearing it."

"It may be months before we get any new clothes."

Her daughter sashayed down the stairs and pranced around, whirling her skirts and wrinkling her small nose, her heart-shaped lips pursed a moment. Then she flopped into one of the stuffed chairs.

"I don't know why Frank has to have his ward out here, anyhow," Emmy Lou said, fluffing her hair. "All he talks about is her. Charity this. Charity that. And she's coming with that awful sister of his, that Nora."

"Just be patient, dear."

"And this is such a terrible place. We had it so much better with your last husband."

"And even better when he died," Elva said.

Emmy Lou smiled. "He was the toughest one, wasn't he? The others went so easy, but not him, and if you think Frank Sladek will be any easier—"

"Hush, dear. Right now I'd love to get into that tin box he keeps locked up. He promised me a will giving me half of everything. But until I see it, we'll be nice to everyone, including Charity."

While Elva and her daughter dreamed of their wealthy future, night fell in the hills to the southeast where Charity was already unsaddling near the edge of camp. Billy had roped in the remuda back in the trees, thirty horses having been recovered, and he was getting around with his sore legs and one good arm without much trouble.

Hooper and his men were sitting around the campfire near the chuck wagon, eating their fill.

Billy looked toward them and spoke softly.

"They're a mean-lookin' bunch, ain't they?"

"Don't worry," she said. "We should be out of here in a few days."

"Bet they was all surprised when you rode out." She smiled as she removed her hat. "You bet they were. And thanks for letting me borrow this."

"No, you keep it. Gives me an excuse to use Tom's new Stetson. And that looks mighty fine on you." His face went red with the compliment.

"Thank you, Billy."

She stayed with him in the moonlight until Hooper and his men rode back to the herd. Then she walked over to the campfire, where the cook was stirring the beans in a big pot hanging from the tripod over the flames.

"Smells good," she said.

"I'm surprised you ain't got a hole in you. Woman out there herdin' cows."

"You too?" she asked, laughing. "I was born to the saddle, you know that. I didn't stop riding just because I went to live with Frank's cousin. She taught me a lot more, you know. Riding and shooting, and even herding sheep."

The cook growled. "Sheep? That does it."

Again she laughed and knelt by the fire, warming her hands as she frowned. "I will admit though, I'm really sore all over. That's hard work out there. My arms are about to fall off, and I'm not sure I can sit down."

"Good. Serves you right."

"But don't you dare tell any of this to Uncle Frank."

"He'll figure it all out for himself."

Billy came over to join them, just as Bronco, Curly, and Tom came riding in. After the horses were cared for, the four men squatted by the fire.

Curly looked gingerly at Charity, who was smiling but still kneeling. "You did all right, girl."

"Bet she can't sit down," Bronco said with a grin.

She made a face as she sipped her coffee. Then she sat down, gritting her teeth behind closed lips, legs crossed in front of her.

"I can out-ride you any day," she said.

"Not Bronco Wade," Billy told her. "He's legend."

Charity smiled. "So we're told. I haven't seen it yet."

"Take my word for it," Curly said.

"The legend sure is hungry," she teased, watching Bronco shovel down his food, embarrassing him.

As they ate, Bronco couldn't help but glance at her often. She sure was something. Firelight danced in her dark hair, and her eyes were shining. That smile and that laugh could sure make a man think twice about roaming. Not that she'd be interested in a saddle tramp.

Tom was talking about the herd. "We got about eighteen hundred I'd say. We did real well. And Miss Charity was a great help."

"We'll be tradin' off around three in the mornin'," Curly said. "So I reckon we'd better get some sleep."

They all rolled into their blankets except Billy and Curly, who were taking first watch. Billy squatted near the chuck wagon, blankets around him and his rifle across his knees, while Curly walked down near the remuda.

Bronco couldn't sleep, and he lay listening to the cattle in the distance and that same lone coyote. He sat up in the glow of the dwindling fire and looked at Charity's lush locks covering her face. The more he looked at her, the lonelier he felt.

Standing, rifle in hand, he decided to relieve Curly.

But before he could move, he heard his buckskin nicker. And he saw a shadow down by the remuda.

FOUR

Signaling Billy to lie low and awaken Tom, Bronco moved into the trees toward the ropes surrounding the remuda. When he was but twenty feet away, he leaned against a tree and went down on one knee. The moonlight was casting heavy shadows from the trees, and there was a terrible stillness. He realized he was holding his breath, and he tried to breathe deep.

His Winchester already cocked with a shell in chamber, he continued to scan the night, watching for movement, praying they would go for the horses instead. And yet Curly was down that way.

There had been twenty Arapaho on the ridge.

Sweat was running down Bronco's back and rear, and his mouth was so dry it was burning, like his lips and throat. His heavy coat felt fiercely hot in the cold night, but his hands were like ice on his rifle.

Then he saw something moving down by the creek, toward Curly's position, but he couldn't see Curly. He was afraid to signal, and he looked around behind him, just in time.

Something big was heaving toward him, tall and muscular and wearing only a breech cloth, and cold steel came slashing down past his neck as he dodged.

Bronco tried to rise, but the big Arapaho was on top of him, and they hit the ground with a thud. He heard other running feet, and he pulled the trigger in warning, the shot going wild.

Dropping his Winchester to grapple the big warrior with both hands, Bronco was breathing hard, chilled to the bone, feeling the man's amazing strength as he fought back. The blade kept slashing near his neck and face, and he had hold of the man's thick wrist, grunting with every thrust.

They rolled across the ground as he heard more shots.

Bronco got his knee up in the Arapaho's gut and pushed, and as they broke apart, he pulled his six-gun, but the Indian was on him again, and his shot went wild. The knife slashed Bronco's right shoulder as they struggled and rolled about.

Bronco managed to fire again, and this time, his bullet went right up into the man's heart. The fierce warrior kept fighting with his last breath, eyes dark and blazing in the moonlight even as he died.

Gasping for air, Bronco got to one knee, ignoring the pain and blood on his right shoulder, and he retrieved his Winchester as he holstered his six-gun. He could see running figures, but he didn't know who was who or what was happening. He couldn't see Charity.

Shots were fired around the camp, and Bronco got up and went running over to it, only to stumble over a dead Arapaho, and then another.

Billy had crawled over to a tree with his rifle, and Tom was kneeling next to Charity, who was holding a six-gun in both hands, all color drained from her face, her body trembling all over. They were alive, and there was no movement around them. Bronco drew a deep breath in relief.

But they heard more shots down by the horses.

"Curly," Bronco muttered.

And he spun fast, running back through the

trees, rifle cocked and ready, his heart pounding as he scanned the shadows; then he saw the horses heading down along the creek at a gallop, all of them, even his buckskin, all herded by Arapaho.

Where was Curly?

Frantic, Bronco ran faster, tripping over brush.

And then he saw two dead Arapaho near Curly, who lay on his back, clasping his left arm and breathing hard. Blood was running hot through his fingers, and there was blood on the side of his head, dribbling down into his red beard.

Bronco was choking on his tears as he knelt.

"They got the horses," Curly moaned.

"It's all right."

"They sure was big Injuns."

"Lets get you back to camp."

Tom was suddenly there, kneeling. "We'll carry you."

Bronco and Tom made a chair of their hands and lifted the dazed and wounded Curly into it. He didn't weigh much, and the two men carried him easily back to the others, who quickly gathered round.

Charity knelt as they lowered Curly onto some blankets. She wiped the blood from his face with a lace handkerchief as he stared up at her. Her hands were quivering.

"Now who should stay in camp?" she asked.

The cook came to care for Curly, whose wounds were superficial, for he suffered most from the blow on his head. Bronco sat back on the ground, suddenly feeling the pain of his torn flesh.

"Bronco," she said, startled. "You're hurt."

"Just a crease."

"You lie down," she ordered.

He didn't mind, and as he lay on his left side, she began to tear his shirt. Her long dark hair was brushing his face, and she smelled mighty nice. He didn't watch her hands, only her wonderful face and long lashes, the way her eyes sometimes caught the moonlight and glittered like emeralds.

The cook came over to finish the cleansing and bandaging. Both wounded men were able to sit up, and they all sat staring at each other, considering their plight.

"Seems mighty funny Hooper and the others didn't come runnin'," Curly said.

Billy turned to Charity. "You probably shot the big one. Was you scared?"

"A little."

Billy grinned. "A little? I bet you wet your britches."

The cook turned with a snort. "That's no way—"

But everyone else was laughing, including Charity, and it relieved the tension and remaining fear. Then Tom and Bronco dragged off the dead Arapaho to bury them.

No one could sleep after that, and they sat having hot coffee and thinking of how close they came to dying.

It was long after three in the morning when they heard the sound of hoofbeats. They moved away from the fire and dropped into the tall, damp grass, listening and waiting, short of breath with hearts beating wild.

And then they saw it, loping toward them and kicking and bucking. It was Bronco's big buckskin, followed by ten ponies, leaving twenty with the Arapaho and long gone.

Bronco got to his feet, ignoring the pain in his shoulder and hurrying forward. The buckskin nosed him and shoved him backward. Bronco stroked the strong jaws and neck, and he was grinning.

"Bucky, you can buck me off anytime, old fella."

Billy and Tom came to gather the other horses into the rope enclosure. The moon was bright but it was mighty cold. They returned to camp and sat down, exhausted.

Now they saw Hooper riding in with Boney and Krinkle.

The cook excitedly told them what happened.

"They got twenty horses," Tom said. "Where were you?"

Hooper leaned on the pommel of his saddle. "We didn't hear nothin'. We was a mile away with them cattle makin' a lot of noise."

"Why didn't you wake us at three?" Bronco asked.

"We couldn't sleep no how," Hooper said, straightening.

Curly was no longer dazed and wanted to be in the saddle despite Charity's protest. Tom elected to stand guard with Billy. Curly and Bronco headed back to the herd to relieve the other men. At first light, they continued their hunt for stragglers.

But Curly was mighty annoyed. "You figure Hooper knew what was goin' on and was hopin' them Injuns would finish us?"

Bronco nodded. "From what Tom said of the stampede, yeah. But Tom told 'em we was only a week from the valley, so I don't think they'll try anything now."

Curly made a face. "We're still in quicksand."

"If I could just be sure them Arapaho wouldn't be back."

"You want to take that chance?"

"No, I was just thinkin'."

"Well, don't think. You weaken the team."

Bronco grinned. "I can see you're feelin' better."

For the next few days, everyone but the cook was in the saddle, struggling to recover as many head as they could.

Then one sunny afternoon, six riders came onto the horizon from the west.

Tom reined up near Curly and Bronco, who were frozen.

"That's Leo Sladek. The big one on the bay. The others are Trigger Bar hands. The one with the silver on his gunbelt and the fancy vest, that's Cord. They say he's fast, but I ain't never seen him do anything."

"What are you goin' to tell 'im?" Curly asked, wiping his brow.

"Everything."

As Tom rode off at a lope toward the distant riders, Bronco drew a deep breath. "Leo was maybe five years older than me."

"Just pray real quick. Anything starts, I'll get the ones on the left, work toward the middle. You take the right."

Bronco turned in the saddle to look down the hill to where Charity was shouting like a cowhand to move the cattle. With her tied-down hat and hair tucked under it, wearing a heavy coat and the riding skirt not clearly discernible from a distance, she could be mistaken for a man, but not for long.

Seeing the visitors on the far rise with Tom, she spun her sorrel and rode up the slope to where Curly and Bronco were watching. Her face was damp with perspiration, and she pushed her hat back from her brow.

"Who are they?"

"Big fellow's Leo Sladek," Bronco said, watching her face and seeing no enthusiasm.

"Oh," she said.

Leo Sladek had a lined, square face with a rather long nose. When he rode up with Tom and his men, he didn't realize it was Charity at first.

Then he grinned. "Well, I'll be. You sure have growed up, Miss Charity. Maybe you remember me always grabbin' your pigtails."

"I remember."

"Now there's a lot more to grab. But Pa sure would have a fit if he could see you right now. We'd better get you cleaned up afore we get to Bear Creek."

She forced a smile. "We needed all the hands we could get."

"I hear you shot an Arapaho."

"I don't know," she said. "It all happened so fast."

"You're a real frontier woman. And you're my pick, all right. Lucas can have that washed-out Emmy Lou."

Bronco glanced past Leo to study Cord, the gunman with the sleazy smile, a man in his thirties with blazing dark eyes and crooked jaw. Cord was giving Bronco the once-over.

She introduced Bronco and Curly, but Leo had never heard of them. She then told of how Bronco had saved her life during the stampede.

"Yeah, well, thanks," Leo said.

His throat dry as dust, Bronco glanced at Curly, both of them sweating heavily under their clothes but realizing Leo didn't have any idea who they were.

"Me and Curly, we'll help you get the herd together and head out in the next day or two."

Leo pushed his hat back. "Well, now, me and the boys, we saw Injun signs. Maybe sixty ponies crossed our trail. You leave, there'll only be a dozen of us to fight 'em off. You fellas look like you can handle them irons. You see us to the main trail, I'll make it worth your while."

Curly and Bronco reined aside as Leo and the others rode toward camp, and Curly wiped his brow with the back of his hand. Both men were badly shaken, and Curly spoke under his breath.

"I got sweat all the way to my boots."

"He didn't recognize us."

"No, but I could feel that rope burn on my neck."

Bronco was grim. "I was figurin' with Leo here, there'd be enough men to get Charity home safe. But sixty ponies, Curly. We can't leave. We're back in the quicksand."

"We get to the main trail, we'll head west."

Back at camp that night, Charity had changed into her velvet jacket. Her hair was combed in large waves about her face. Leo made sure he was sitting next to her by the fire. Hooper had come in and was making a show of his hard work, while his men stayed with the herd.

Bronco was getting annoyed at Leo's attentions to Charity, and he got up and walked down to the creek, rifle under his arm, watching the shadows in the moonlight. It wasn't likely the Arapaho would wander back this way, but he was being mighty careful.

He leaned on a cottonwood and stared at the crystal clear stream in the moonlight, his thoughts on the past and staying alive. He was there nearly half an hour before he heard a soft voice.

"Bronco?"

He turned to see Charity coming down through the trees, and he stiffened. "You shouldn't be out here."

"They're asleep, except for Billy. Can I talk to you?"

He shrugged. "Sure."

She moved to stand near him, her arms wrapped about herself in the chill. Even in Billy's wool coat, she was gorgeous in the moonlight. He wanted to turn tail and run, but all he could do was lean on the cottonwood and gaze at her with as much indifference as he could muster.

"We're almost home," she said.

"Been a tough trip for you."

"But with you and Curly here, it's been kind of nice. It tickles me when he acts like a father."

"He's mighty fond of you."

"You said once you have no family. How old were you when you lost them?"

"My mother died when I was born. My pa, when I was fourteen. But Curly's been lookin' after me a long time."

She gazed up at the stars. "The sky is so close here.

Don't you feel it? As if we could reach up and touch the stars."

Bronco swallowed hard, and they fell silent, gazing from the little creek to the roll of the land and the vast"splendor of the starry sky. It was mighty pleasant standing near her.

Then she glanced at him. "Leo seems nice enough."

"I reckon."

"You're not helping me."

"What do you want me to say?"

"That he's an awful man."

"Is he?"

She shook her head. "I don't know. Miss Freddie, who raised me in Kentucky, she said the Sladeks killed people all the time. I don't know what to believe."

"Then I reckon you're gonna have to see for yourself."

She turned and gazed up at him in the chill of the pale light, her eyes wide and glistening. "Curly says you're a good friend. That you can be trusted."

He shivered as she moved closer. "Reckon so."

"I've been protected and shielded. No men were ever allowed to call on me. Those were Uncle Frank's orders. And now I'm twenty-five years old."

To his consternation, her hand was on his arm.

His face was hot, burning, and he looked away.

"In a short time, I'll be at the Trigger Bar. And I'll be married to a stranger. It'll be a cold and friendless beginning, and I need something nice to remember. My first kiss, from a friend. Please, Bronco?"

He couldn't look at her, and he couldn't move.

After a long, breathless moment, she dropped her hand from his arm and turned slowly away toward camp.

But Bronco came to life and caught her by

the waist from behind, holding her and slowly turning her toward him with his left hand, his right still holding the Winchester. She felt small but alive all over, her head only as high as his chin.

As she looked up at him with that incredible face and those large, shining eyes, he felt his heart swelling, and he hurt down to his boots. Sweat covered his back, and his mouth was so dry, it burned.

Her fingers went up his coat to the collar, and he could feel her soft breath on his hot neck. She lifted her face as he held her gently, and she closed her eyes.

He drew a deep breath and bent down to press his dry lips to her sweet, moist ones, and his heart shriveled away. His knees buckled, but he kept kissing her and kissing her. His hands fell away from her, and yet he couldn't draw his lips from hers.

She was kissing him back for a long moment.

Then she fell away, gazing up at him with awe. Bronco tried to swallow, but his mouth was dry, and he hurt all over. He could barely stand and had trouble catching his breath. He was a disaster.

Suddenly, she giggled. "That was fun."

All he could do was stand like an idiot while she giggled again and turned to go back to camp. That was the gigglingest girl he'd ever met. She moved away in the night, and he leaned on the tree, wiping his brow.

And then he was startled by a low voice. "Bronco."

"Curly, where'd you come from?"

"What are you doin' kissin' my daughter?"

"She kissed me."

"Yeah? Why?"

"Said she'd never been kissed before. And she didn't want a Sladek to be the first."

"Well, you ain't much better."

"You're actin' like a father, Curly, and she knows it. You're gonna give yourself away."

"Well, I can't help it."

Bronco pushed his hat back. "I reckon we can see 'em to the stage road like we planned, then head south from there. But you'd better watch yourself around Leo. He might start gettin' ideas and rememberin'."

Curly folded his arms and shifted his weight, his red beard twitching and green eyes brimming. "Twenty-three years ago, she was a two-year-old with big eyes and pug nose. Used to put her arms around my neck and give me a big wet kiss. Now she's gettin' married to a Sladek."

"And there's nothin' you can do about it."

"I know."

They stayed by the creek awhile, unaware that Leo had awakened long enough to see Charity return and crawl into her blankets. As she slept Leo sat up with a silent snarl, and he threw his own covers aside, then got up and walked over to where Lazlo was snoring on the other side of the campfire.

Later in the night, Bronco and Curly returned to camp. Leo Sladek was lying on his back with his head on his saddle and hat over his face. He was snoring and whistling.

Charity was lying half-covered by her blankets. She awakened as Curly knelt to pull her covers up and to add one of his own blankets. She smiled up at him.

"You're so nice, Curly. Why aren't you married?"

"I was, but she died."

"I'm sorry."

She reached up to squeeze his arm, then settled back in her blankets and closed her eyes. Curly sat back on his heels, his face void of color.

At first light over breakfast with several of the hands gathered round, Bronco was downing his coffee when Leo turned to him. "I'll bet we got a horse you can't ride."

"That so?"

"Yep. Old Trigger Foot, they call him. We keep 'im around for the fun of it. Pa would pay a hundred dollars to anyone who can, but that horse is gonna die of old age before that. He's goin' on six now."

"Well, we ain't got time to go to the Trigger Bar."

Charity looked up from her coffee, her face strained. "But I don't want you to leave, Bronco. You saved my life."

"We're headed for Oregon, by way of Butte City."

"Butte City," one of the cowhands said. "They got hurdy-gurdy dance halls and a couple breweries and plenty of saloons."

"I won't have it," she said with a stubborn lift of her chin. "Bronco Wade, you cannot leave until… until you ride Trigger Foot."

"Maybe he's afraid," Leo said. "Doesn't want to ruin his reputation."

Curly scratched his beard. "Ain't no horse Bronco can't ride, but we got plans."

"Bronco?" she asked.

Bronco looked at the urgency in her face and gleaming eyes. She was silently begging him to go to the Trigger Bar. Curly was sitting with his hands clasped, staring at them.

"Sorry," Bronco said. "We've already stayed too long. We get to the stage road, we're headin' out."

She frowned, then walked over to talk to the cook. Curly and Bronco exchanged glances.

Bronco sipped his coffee, then stared into the rising steam. It was a mighty curious situation. Two men were held in quicksand by a single little woman.

But the next morning, watching first light caressing her dark red hair, he figured she *might* be worth a hanging. She was still sleeping, but the men were up and around, and Hooper and Lazlo had come in for breakfast. Curly and Bronco were sitting side by side, enjoying bacon and beans and new biscuits.

Bronco needed more coffee and set his plate down, just as dirt was kicked into it.

Pushing his hat back, he looked up at Lazlo, the man's flat nose seeming to puff a little as he snickered.

"You got a problem?" Bronco asked.

"Yeah, I don't like your face."

"You want to do somethin' about it?"

Lazlo's near-white eyes narrowed and darkened. "Yeah."

Leo looked up. "Away from the fire, boys."

Bronco set his cup down and stood up. He was plenty tall, but he only came to Lazlo's shoulder height. He looked up at the big shoulders and saw the huge hands spread out and waiting.

The sun was brightening the camp as they both stepped away from the fire, some five feet apart, and Bronco allowed as how the man's reach was more than that. Lazlo was rippling his muscles and grinning. They could hear men taking bets in the background.

Lazlo sneered, lips curling back from crooked teeth.

"Come and get it."

FIVE

As Bronco and Lazlo slowly moved in a circle, watching each other, hands lifted, the others moved back, and Charity was awakened.

It was still cold, and the sun had yet to rise over the distant hills, but it was light. The earth smelled of dew and wet sod, and there was no wind.

Bronco felt hot sweat on his back, running down his rear. His heart was racing, his blood was cold, and his knees were a little unsteady. Something was telling him this big oaf was going to beat the dickens out of him.

"Come on," Lazlo said. "I want to see what legends are made of."

"You got a glass jaw and soft belly," Bronco said. "You'd better quit while you're ahead."

"I'm gonna break you in half and hang you up for the buzzards."

"Afore you do, you got some reason?"

Lazlo nodded, chuckling, but he didn't answer, and he kept circling Bronco. Now the big man was coming closer, reaching.

Bronco danced backward and around, fists ready, but watching those huge hands. Suddenly, Lazlo swung so hard his knuckles whistled as they skimmed Bronco's cheek, but he missed as Bronco danced aside.

"Stay still, legend."

As Lazlo swung again, Bronco fainted with his left and plowed his right into the man's gut. Lazlo gasped, doubling up and falling back before he could catch his breath.

But it had only made Lazlo mad, and he charged like a wild bull. Bronco jumped aside and tripped him, and Lazlo went hurtling across the grass like a bullet, slamming into a tree, smashing his hat and leaving him on his knees, stunned.

Bronco breathed a sigh of relief, but it was too soon.

Lazlo got to his feet, still shaken, but furious.

And the big man spun around and charged again.

This time he was quick on his feet and plunged into Bronco dead center. The two of them crashed backward onto the dirt, the man's weight like a boulder on Bronco's chest.

Oof! Bronco gasped.

Lazlo's hands were suddenly at his throat, choking the life from him. Bronco grabbed his wrists, but they were like iron. Dazed as he fought the man's great weight and the death grip on his throat, Bronco tried to stay conscious.

Then Bronco let go and slammed his fist onto the man's flat nose, again and again, the way you'd fight a grizzly.

Lazlo let go and fell off of him, moaning and holding his face and nose, frantic as blood ran through his fingers.

"You broke my nose!"

Bronco rolled away from him and got to one knee, trying to get his strength back. He could still feel those big hands choking the life from him, and he was aware of the others standing near the fire and watching. There was no way he could just consider the fight over, not if he wanted to keep his pride.

Hands in front of him, breathing hard, Bronco spoke as gruff as he could manage. "You about through?"

Lazlo sat up, pulling his bandanna and holding it to his nose. "Women like my nose all the time. Makes me handsome. Now look what you done."

"Are you through?"

"This time, yeah. But I'm still gonna finish you, legend. I'm gonna bury you myself."

Bronco drew a cool breath and got to his feet, trying not to stagger. He walked back toward the campfire as Leo and Hooper passed him to get to Lazlo.

Leo knelt by the big man and mumbled, "You just blew fifty dollars."

"I ain't finished," Lazlo muttered.

"Make sure it's in front of her."

"I'll get 'im. Don't worry."

"I could get you all hanged for what you tried to do with the herd," Leo said, "but I ain't gonna tell my pa nothin' because I need you fellas around. But you'd better do as I say."

"We're with you all the way," Hooper said.

While the three men spoke softly Bronco moved to the campfire and sat down clumsily next to Curly. He was hurting all over and still had trouble breathing.

"You all right?" Curly asked.

"Almost."

"I won fifty dollars on you."

"Thanks."

Charity came to kneel in front of Bronco. "He could have killed you."

"I was gonna beat him silly," Bronco said.

Charity smiled."Sure looked like it, all right."

Bronco grinned and removed his bandanna to wipe his sweaty face. Then he watched as Lazlo limped back to the other side of the campfire with Hooper while Leo came over to Bronco and stood looking down at him.

"Well, you got through that one."

Bronco made a face. "There's more?"

Leo grinned. "That's up to Lazlo, ain't it?"

"Just checking."

"Come, Charity, sit by me," Leo said, taking her hand and pulling her to her feet, then leading her away from Bronco.

Later, as the men returned to hunting down strays, Lazlo was riding with a bandage across his nose and face. Krinkle rode over to Bronco in the afternoon and reined up beside him with a chuckle.

"Lazlo's bound to kill you."

"I reckon he'll try. What set him off?"

"Leo offered him fifty dollars."

"Why?"

"Seems Leo saw Miss Charity comin' back from the creek where you was. He didn't like that much. But you saved her life, so he can't run you off. He has to look like he's bein' nice to you so Charity will think he's a fine fellow. But he figures to have Lazlo mash you to a pulp first and bury you later. And if that don't work, he's still got Cord."

"That's real nice," Bronco said.

Krinkle grinned, wiping his brow. "Well, back to work. Only thing you can count on in this life is cows. They's always the same."

Two days later, with the cattle mostly gathered up, the herd began to move northwest toward the blue mountains. Charity insisted on riding, and Leo took it on himself to stay with her. It was a cold, brisk morning with a clear sky and dew on the grass.

As they rode he glanced at her often.

"You really are somethin'. There's gonna be one big fight over you."

"Uncle Frank said I was to do the choosing."

"You'll be pickin' the winner, that's all."

"What makes you think it'll be you?"

He grinned. "Cause I'm the biggest."

One of his men signaled him, and he rode off, leaving her to draw a deep breath. And she was pleased as Curly came riding up beside her.

"That Leo giving you any trouble?"

"No, Curly, but thanks for asking."

"Maybe you oughta go back to Kentucky."

She shook her head. "I have no choice."

"So you're really going to marry a Sladek?"

"They're the only ones who ever cared about me. My own family threw me away when I was two. Frank Sladek looked after me, and when I was ten, he sent me to live with his cousin's widow, Miss Freddie, so I could go to school."

Curly winced at her words. "Could be your folks just couldn't take care of you. Maybe they was sick, or had no money and was starvin'. You can't judge 'em without knowin'. And they did leave you in a church."

"How did you know that?"

"Uh, I heard it from the cook."

"I guess you're right. But I always felt unwanted, except for Uncle Frank. He's gruff, but I can twist him around my little finger. Anyway, he insisted I be educated. That's why I went with Miss Freddie to Kentucky."

"You didn't learn to ride like that in no finishin' school."

She smiled. "No, I didn't. She bought a sheep

ranch and a few head of cattle. And she raises horses now. And she used to be a schoolteacher, so she taught me at home, but we worked the ranch together. If Uncle Frank finds out she took his money and used it for the ranch instead of school, he'll have a fit."

"She sounds all right."

She turned serious. "Freddie was wonderful. But Uncle Frank sent his sister to bring me for marriage to one of his sons. I didn't want to come right away, but Nora threatened to tell on Freddie, get her sent to jail and have her ranch taken away. So here I am."

"Sounds like a mean woman, that Nora."

"Freddie doesn't know why I left. I think she would have given up the ranch to stop me, but I couldn't let that happen."

"But only Mrs. Paulson knew, isn't that right?"

"Thank you, Curly, but it's too late to turn back. Besides, I'm nearly a spinster. It's time I married, and there's nothing wrong with pleasing Uncle Frank. Not after all he's done for me."

Curly bit his lip, stopping the anger that was rising in his throat. Yeah, Sladek had done a lot, all right. He had used the new tax laws to steal their land with the help of carpetbaggers, and when her mother died, began hunting her father like an animal.

As they rode side by side, Curly felt an agony he could scarcely contain. This was his little girl, all grown up, and he couldn't even tell her who he was. Nor could he interfere. It was tearing his heart out.

The last night on the trail before they reached Bear Creek Valley, Curly and Bronco rode around the herd, whistling and singing to calm the cattle, but they soon reined up in the moonlight.

"Bronco, it's drivin' me crazy."

"Then tell her."

"Tell her what? That I was a rustler the Sladeks tried to hang?"

Bronco pushed his hat back from his damp brow. "Brandin' mavericks ain't no crime."

"Them Sladek boys called it rustling."

Bronco grinned. "If I hadn't come along, your neck would've stretched clear to the Rio Grande."

"I tell you, Bronco. You were a real sight comin' over that ridge, a skinny little kid on a mule with that old Henry repeater. Them three Sladeks was laughin' when you hauled down on 'em, but they tried to blow your head off. To this day, I ain't figured how you got all three. And you was shot full of holes."

"But you saved my life."

"Well, maybe I'm bein' ungrateful after all these years, but why did you save mine?"

Bronco shrugged. "That's how my father died. Somebody hanged him. I found him a day later. And he weren't no rustler. I never did find out who done it, but the Sladeks got our land right after. I was only fourteen, and I took off, figurin' I'd be next."

"I'll be switched. You never told me how your pa died."

"It hurt too bad, and later, I just bottled it up."

Curly wiped his eyes. "So when you saw me—"

"I had to do somethin'."

"You been carryin' that hurt all these years."

"What hurts is not knowin' who done it."

Curly started to speak, then thought better of it. Both men had their ghosts to deal with, and it was painful enough without talking about it.

But Bronco's ghost hovered in his thoughts. He had loved his father, his mother having died in childbirth, and the two of them had done everything together. They had been friends as well as father and son. He still had the nightmares of finding him dangling from a cottonwood. It was unlikely he would ever learn who murdered him.

That night was the last on the trail before they reached the stage road in the valley. They were deep in the rolling hills and scattered woods. The grass was tall and green, and the cattle were regaining some of the weight they had lost.

There had been no sign of the Arapaho or any Sioux. Just a few Crows trading for a head of beef. Jackrabbits darted from the brush. Buzzards sailed overhead to look them over. Mule deer tracks crossed their trail. And at night, they heard another lone coyote's mournful wail.

One of the young cowboys with Leo had a harmonica and was playing lively tunes around the campfire while Billy sang a song he had written himself:

> *"I lost my rope and fell off my horse,*
> *And sat on a prickly pear,*
> *The old cow charged and I ran like heck,*
> *And jumped in the big creek there,*
> *Well, I can't swim, so I holler loud,*
> *And she comes right after me,*
> *So I learned to jump like any old frog,*
> *Right up in a hollow tree,*

But the tree falls down and carries me,
Right up to the Pearly Gate,
And St. Peter says get out of here,
Cause we didn't have no date—"

Everyone laughed at Billy's story songs.

When the others were asleep, Charity was alone with Bronco and Curly by the flickering firelight.

She was teasing Bronco as usual. "Tell me, legend, do you really think you can ride that Trigger Foot? Or do you want me to go first?"

Curly laughed, and Bronco leaned back on his saddle with a grin, but when he lay in his blankets that night, staring at the stars, his heart was heavy with bitter sadness. He had not been sorry for those grand years with Curly, but he would never get over the loss of his father. Yet how he longed to close that part of his life and take another look at this silly girl who was getting to him.

In the morning, Charity was again teasing Bronco. Not Billy or Tom or Curly, and certainly not Leo, who was always frowning. When Leo was riding with Cord, the gunman smiled.

"Leo, I can read your face."

"That Bronco's gettin' away with too much.

We get to the valley, that's all gonna change."

"I thought that's where he and Curly were leavin' us."

"I don't want her pinin' over some bronc buster. I want him dead or humiliated, or both."

"Want me to take 'im?"

"Think you can?"

"Easy."

"Let's see what Lazlo does first."

SIX

By late afternoon, Bronco and Curly were on the ridge ahead of the others. Below, a vast emerald valley spread for many miles in all directions, crossed with crystal streams and dotted with pines and cottonwoods. On the far horizons, there were blue mountains. The well-traveled stage road ran north and south.

"Lord a'mighty," Curly said softly.

"I'd like a piece of that," Bronco murmured.

"Reckon Sladek's got most of it by now."

"Don't matter. We get the herd down there, and we head out first light tomorrow. Remember?"

"We got no choice."

Long-suppressed hatred was burning in Curly's gaze.

While the herd was being moved into the

valley by late evening, Frank Sladek was pulling off his boots near the hearth in his big house. The smell was of sweat and dirt.

Elva sweetly took up his boots and set them aside. She brought him his pipe as he leaned back in his big leather chair. As he lit it, she sat near him on the couch and smiled with affection.

"They'll be here soon, Elva."

"Who, dear?"

"The herd. And Charity. One of the boys rode ahead to tell me."

"Oh, that's just wonderful. I'll be sure their rooms are ready."

"My sister was killed in a stampede."

"That dear Nora? Oh, I'm so sorry, Frank."

"You'll have to take charge of Charity."

"Of course, dear."

But Elva's mind was churning crazily, and she could hardly wait to race upstairs to tell Emmy Lou.

"Oh, mother, I'm glad that terrible Nora's gone, but I was hoping Charity would never come. She could very well get in the way. Frank dotes on her so."

"We never let anyone in our way for long, darling."

Emmy Lou smiled. "That's right."

While the women talked upstairs, Frank's other son, Lucas, came in from the chill of night. He was a good-sized man with a thin nose and a thin, swarthy face. He sat by the fire and looked at his father, who was opening his eyes to squint at him.

"Pa, I figure at least ten of them mares are in foal."

"That's good. But we'll be gettin' our own stud one of these days."

"But somethin' else, Pa. Leo will be back plenty soon with Charity. And we'll both be gettin' hitched. It ain't right we'll still be nothin' but hired hands. Leo's gonna be forty in five years, and I'll catch up a year later."

"I told you. When I figure you're both ready, you'll each get one-third. Right now you'll each keep on gettin' 5 percent of the profits."

"But with us gettin' married—"

"It's enough."

"But with the last herd comin', you'll have nearly twenty thousand head in Montana. That's enough for all three of us divided up right now. It's our right, Pa."

"Don't give me no trouble, Lucas. I ain't changin' my mind."

"But if somethin' happened to you afore then,

your new wife could get it all."

"Ain't so."

"But it seems to me—"

"Don't think too hard, Lucas. It makes your eyes squint. I got my will all set, and the original's with our lawyer in Austin. All you got to know is, you and Leo are gonna get everything. Elva can go back east and find someone else."

"She's countin' on more."

"As long as I'm around, she's got me. That's enough."

"I figured she had her hooks in you."

Frank stared into the fire. "Only one woman ever had me that crazy."

"Ma?"

"No, after your ma died. A woman I could never have, that's what. Now what else you got to talk about?"

"That cowboy that brought the news, he said Charity was the most beautiful woman he'd ever seen. That she works cattle like a man and rides like a Comanche."

"So?"

"Me and Leo, we're both gonna want her instead of that simpering Emmy Lou."

"Then flip a coin. What's the big deal?"

"Leo's already out there courtin'. It ain't fair."

Frank Sladek reached for his pipe with a grin. "About time we had some fun around here."

"Somethin' else, Pa. Two fellas showed up on the drive. One's Bronco Wade, braggin' how he was breakin' broncs all over Wyomin' Territory and never been throwed."

"And?"

"He was makin' cow eyes at Charity. So we oughta have him try old Trigger Foot. We can have a big party and barbecue to celebrate Charity's comin', and have a band and do some dancin', and invite the townsfolk. And make a fool of this Bronco Wade at the same time."

Frank was thoughtful. "Not a bad idea. Elva's been after me to socialize some. We can introduce Charity to these folks around here."

While Lucas and his father were talking, Leo was sitting around the campfire with Charity, Hooper, and Lazlo, along with Cord. The others were night herding. Hooper was wolfing down his food while the cook made faces at him.

"Lazlo," Leo said, "are you gonna let Bronco bluff you?"

"I ain't finished with him."

"He'll whup you again," Hooper said.

Charity was distressed, setting down her cup. "Leo, please do not allow any more fighting."

"Don't worry, honey, we'll do it away from camp."

"Do what?"

"Men have to fight, Charity."

"They do not."

Leo frowned. "You're just a woman, so stay out of it."

Cord looked up from his plate. "That's no way to talk to a lady."

"Never mind," Leo said, glaring at him but not quite ready to take him on. "She just don't understand how it is out here. Men have to prove themselves."

"That's a stupid way to do it," she said.

Leo's anger flushed his face red, and he swallowed his hot words as she stood up and went over to where her blankets were spread under the chuck wagon.

As Lazlo and Hooper tightened the cinches to return to the herd, Bronco and Curly came riding in for the night. When Bronco started to dismount, Lazlo grabbed him from behind, big hands digging into his gunbelt and jerking him free of the stirrup, then throwing him like a sack of grain to the dirt.

Bronco rolled and got to one knee, just as Lazlo came charging like a bull, head down and snorting. Unable to get out of the way, Bronco took the full weight of the tall man, and they crashed backward with Bronco underneath, knocking the wind out of him.

Squirming under the man's weight and pounding fists, Bronco managed to slam the palm of his hand against Lazlo's sore nose.

Lazlo gasped in pain and rolled off, grabbing his nose.

As both men got to their knees, Bronco slammed his right fist into Lazlo's gut. As the man doubled up, Bronco punched him in the jaw hard with his left, snapping Lazlo's head back and nearly breaking Bronco's hand.

Lazlo roared like a lion as Bronco got up and danced away. Staggering to his feet, Lazlo went to his full height with blood trickling from his nose.

"I'm gonna kill you, Bronco."

"Stop it!"

They both looked into the barrel of a Winchester held level at the cheek of Charity Sladek and gripped tight and sure in her slim hands. Her eyes were blazing.

"Get away from each other."

Lazlo laughed, pushing his hat back. "Hah."

She fired, and his hat went sailing into the

night. Lazlo gasped, feeling his head to be sure it was there.

"You're a crazy woman!"

"Next time, it'll be dead center," she said.

Bronco was startled. "Stay out of this."

She turned the weapon toward him. He grabbed his Stetson and took it off, holding it to his chest, eyes wide in disbelief.

"I've had enough of this," she said fiercely. "Lazlo, you get out to the herd. Bronco, you eat and go to bed."

Hooper, sitting in the saddle now, was grinning and laughing. Lazlo, holding his nose with one hand, picked up his hat and stuck his finger through the hole.

"You near killed me," he complained loudly.

She was suddenly aware of Leo coming up behind her, and she spun, backing away so that all were in her sights. Leo stopped, shaking his head.

"Charity, this is man's doing."

"And that's why it's going to stop right now."

"If we was hitched, I'd whup you good."

Curly swung down from the saddle. "Not while I'm around."

Hooper was still chuckling as Lazlo mounted. The two men rode out of camp while the cook hurriedly called Curly and Bronco to supper. Charity was so angry, she didn't talk to anyone and went to her blankets; Leo grimly went to saddle up, muttering to himself. Curly was grinning from ear to ear, and Bronco was counting his blessings.

"She could have got me," he murmured.

"An ear at a time," Curly whispered proudly.

Later, as first light of morning crossed the valley, Curly, Bronco, and the Tyree brothers were down at the remuda.

"Sure is a big sky," Billy said. "Makes you mighty close to God. I wonder what He thinks of us about now."

Tom grunted. "He don't like you wearin' my new Stetson."

"Hey, it fits," Billy said with a laugh.

"We got to say good-bye," Curly told them.

"You write us where you light," Tom urged.

They shook hands, and the Tyree brothers, though unhappy at their leaving, thanked Bronco again for saving Billy's life, then mounted and headed back to the herd.

Bronco groomed his buckskin, deep in thought.

Curly pulled burrs from his bay's tail, then turned.

"Well, let's saddle up. We got to tell 'er we're leavin'."

Bronco put on the blanket and set the saddle, then went to pull up the cinch, but his buckskin had inflated itself like a balloon. Curly laughed, but Bronco growled.

"Dag nab it, Bucky's back to his old tricks. Swellin' up to make the cinch loose."

Bronco shoved his shoulder into the horse's belly, and the animal let out the air with a toss of its head. Quickly he tightened the cinch.

"Yeah," Curly said, "but now he's going to get even."

"It figures. Well, let's get it over with."

They led their horses back to the campfire. Some of the Sladek men were still there, gulping down their coffee. Leo was out with the others, the herd being north of camp, and Charity was helping the cook clean up.

She turned, smiling. "We're almost there."

Curly cleared his throat, then went to the chuck wagon bin for their possibles. She watched in silence as Bronco made up their bedrolls and added some hardtack and other grub from the cook.

"Please, Bronco," she said at last. "Can't you stay a little longer?"

He straightened, turned to tie down the bedrolls, and then shook his head. Curly tied down the possibles, and then both faced her, hearts aching at the tears in her eyes.

"Hey," Curly said. "None of that. We don't never say good-bye to a pretty girl. We'll be back someday."

She fell into Curly's arms, and they hugged each other. Then she leaned back in his embrace and stroked his beard. Standing on her tiptoes, she kissed him on the cheek.

"I love you, Curly."

Curly could only kiss her cheek in return. Then he backed away, his eyes wet.

Leaving Curly a wreck, she turned slowly to the shy, uneasy Bronco. "I love you too, Bronco. You saved my life. I hope you come back to see me."

"Yeah, we will."

She moved toward him, and his heart skipped a dozen beats as she slid into his arms. She hugged him, and he had to hug her back. She felt so small and defenseless against him, and he hated leaving her, but he had to get Curly out of here alive.

Reaching up with her slim fingers to his neck, she pulled his head down. He stared into her glistening emerald eyes, and he was so shattered, he didn't resist as she brought his lips close to hers.

He swallowed hard, and then he kissed her, and kissed her, and kissed her again, and she kept kissing him back.

Out of breath, they broke apart, and he released her.

She stumbled back, hands at her throat. "Please come back, both of you."

"You're gettin' married," Curly said. "You won't miss us."

"I'll always miss you."

Curly and Bronco swung into the saddle, took one last look at her and the waving cook, then headed south along the stage road, away from the camp and the herd, afraid to look back.

"Well," Curly said, choking on his words, "we got out of the quicksand."

Bronco wiped his eyes. "We're still alive."

"But I sure ain't a happy fella."

"Me neither."

SEVEN

Three days later, the two men reached the main trail leading west where it joined the stage road. Broken wagons and several wheels lay in the grass. It was wide open country, green and splendid under a clear evening sky.

There was a relay station with corrals and a white house at the crossing. The stage was sitting in front, a high, rocking vehicle that worked as a torture chamber, luggage heaped on top.

Two men were leading the team into the corral for a change, and one, a scrawny little man, turned around, squinting up at them.

"Howdy, strangers. Light in for some grub. There's plenty of stew. My wife's a good cook. I'm Peters."

"Thanks. I'm Bronco, and this here's Curly.

The stage overnight here?"

"Yeah."

"You got passengers?"

"A couple peddlers and a good-lookin' woman."

"Suits us," Bronco said.

"No room inside," the old man said, "but you can bunk in the barn if you've a mind to."

"Thanks."

They rode over to the tall hay barn and dismounted, leading their horses inside to unsaddle.

At the house, they found a long towel nailed to the wall outside the front door. There was a bowl and a pitcher of water, along with a bar of soap. They gladly washed up, and they turned as the relay man and the stage guard joined them.

Inside the frame house, there was a long table with bowls of food and plates of biscuits, along with a stack of cups and a big pot of steaming hot coffee. The two peddlers were bursting out of their store-bought, pinstriped suits, their faces red as they ate hungrily. The bearded driver was sitting in a chair in the comer, sound asleep.

The woman had a broken feather on her hat, brown curly hair out of place, and a blue travel cape all crushed and rumpled. In her early fifties, she had a good face with large blue eyes and strong chin.

"This here's Mrs. Sladek," Peters said. "Bronco and Curly."

Bronco caught his breath and looked at Curly. It couldn't be another Sladek. They tipped their hats and sat down across from her, staring.

"What's the matter, boys?" she asked. "Haven't you ever seen a woman out here?"

"You're Mrs. Sladek?" Curly asked.

"Don't hold it against me. I've been widowed a long time." She glanced at Bronco for a long moment. "Do I know you from somewhere?"

Bronco squirmed. "No, but are you from Kentucky?"

"Sure am."

"You're Freddie Sladek?" Bronco asked.

"Yes, how did you know? Do you work for that nasty Frank Sladek at Bear Creek?"

"No, ma'am."

"Well, I'm going there to help a young lady as fast as I can."

"Charity?" Curly asked.

"You fellows sure know a lot."

"We met up with the herd she was travelin' with," Curly said. "Headed for the Trigger Bar."

"Yes, that terrible Nora Paulson was with her."

"Mrs. Paulson was killed in a stampede," Bronco said.

Freddie stared at them, setting her fork down slowly. "Is Charity all right?"

"We left her and the herd south of Bear Creek," Curly told her. "Leo Sladek was there."

"She's doing everything they want because of threats to put me in jail. And I won't have it."

Bronco and Curly grinned at each other.

The two curious peddlers stopped eating, their ruddy faces attentive, and Freddie stopped talking. The relay man started the conversation again.

"That new Marshal Norton, he's been arrestin' folks right and left. Takin' 'em to Helena for trial and lockin' 'em up in Deer Lodge."

"Glad to hear that," one peddler said.

"You fellas bring any news with you?"

"They got a big problem with grasshoppers back in Nebraska," the second peddler said. "Why, they're so huge, them things can carry off a cow."

"That's nothin'," the first peddler said. "I seen a lawyer buildin' up a horseless carriage back in New York. Darndest thing you ever saw."

"That's nothin'," the other peddler said. "I was there a year ago when Federal troops come out to quell one of those railroad strikes. Near got my head busted."

After they were no longer able to top each other, the first peddler turned to Miss Freddie. "You sure you won't buy one of those new corsets I got? Why, the Lady Dufferin is only one dollar."

She made a face. "No, thank you."

The second peddler turned to the relay man. "You sure you don't want to buy some white wine vinegar? It's guaranteed for pickles. I got samples."

Curly and Bronco could stand it no longer and went outside into the night air, breathing deep in the silence, sipping their coffee.

"Glory be," Curly said. "Freddie's here to save the day. I sure don't have to worry about Charity now. She'll tear the whole place apart, that one. What a woman."

Bronco grinned. "Yeah, and she's a widow."

"Don't look at me."

They paused as the door opened, and Freddie came outside, drawing her cape about her and insisting on hearing the whole story of the drive. When they were finished, she sat on the bench against the side of the house.

"I took the train to Utah Territory and caught the coach at Corinne. I've been jerked, kicked, and bounced around ever since. I won't be right for a week."

Curly studied her. "You're goin' to have a fight with Frank Sladek, if you're interferin'."

"That Paulson woman, she wrote me a letter after she took Charity away. Told me the only reason Charity went so easy was to keep me out of jail. Frank sent me money for fancy schooling, but I taught her myself and used the money for the ranch. Nora wrote that she was going to write Frank before they ever got to Montana and get me arrested. She was a mean woman."

Curly frowned in the starlight. "If he gets her letter, Frank could still cause you trouble."

"I'm not afraid of him. Oh, he owned half of Texas and now I suppose he has half of Montana. But let me tell you how he got all that money and cattle."

Bronco and Curly sat on their heels, listening.

"The Sladeks just hanged anyone that got in their way, trying to make it look like they were all rustlers. Like the Hemet brothers. And Finnegan. And that Rad Hodges who had all that water. No wonder his son killed three Sladeks."

Bronco choked on his coffee, bringing tears to his eyes. He was glad it was so dark. His heart was pounding so crazily he thought it would break from his chest. He knew Curly was watching him as his face went white.

"Jim Hodges disappeared," Freddie added.

"You have no love for the Sladeks," Curly said, "but you married one."

"A schoolteacher cousin of theirs. He died long before I took Charity east with me. It was his money that bought the ranch, and Frank's that kept it going."

"Do you know who hanged Rad Hodges?" Bronco asked.

Freddie gazed at him a long moment, then shook her head. "I have no proof. Except my friend Whit Hensley said one of the Sladek hands was bragging that Frank and his boys had done it. He didn't know the man's name. Did you know Rad Hodges?"

Bronco swallowed hard. "No. Where is this Hensley?"

"Dead, I'm afraid. They found him in an alley, shot in the back. I guess he knew too much."

She stood up slowly, and the men got to their feet. She put her hand on Bronco's arm, and he backed away. She kept moving toward him, and he continued to retreat. She reached up with her hand and twisted his face sideways into the starlight.

"My land. It's little Jimmy Hodges."

"Quiet," Curly muttered.

She smiled and squeezed Bronco's arm. "Little Jimmy. You don't remember me, do you? I taught you up to the third grade before I was married. You liked throwing spitballs and stuffing things in little girls' inkwells. I had to spank you so many times, I had a sore hand. I noticed you a lot after that, riding like an Indian."

Bronco was so devastated, he didn't know whether to laugh or fall apart.

Curly came over to her, taking her arm and turning her away from Bronco. "Ma'am, you tell anyone that, and he'll be killed faster'n you can finish talkin'."

"Well, I never believed that story about a Hodges gang, so you'd better tell me what happened."

Curly swallowed hard and led her back to the bench, sitting beside her while Bronco stood back aways. Curly explained how he had been branding mavericks and the three older Sladek boys were about to hang him.

"Little Jimmy, I mean Bronco, came over the hill with his old Henry rifle and tried to stop it. They started shootin', and he got all three."

Freddie put her hands to her face. "My land. And Jimmy never could dot an i properly or cross his t's. Or hit anything with a spitball."

"So Bronco here, he was full of bullet holes but he cut me down, and I took him away and hid him out."

"So you must be Wiley Haines, hiding under that beard."

"I'm afraid so, ma'am."

"Come here, Jimmy."

Bronco hesitated, then came to sit on the other side of her. "Don't call me that, Miss Freddie. Don't even tell Charity about this. You'll get us killed."

"All right, Bronco." She squeezed his hand. "Your secret's safe with me. Now how long has Charity been in Bear Creek?"

"About three days."

"And it'll take me near that long to get there. But' you boys had better keep going."

"Not now," Bronco said.

Curly became highly anxious. "Bronco, you can't go back there. You got no proof."

"I'll go to work for Sladek. Someone is bound to talk."

"Leo will have you shot or killed just for being Bronco Wade. He knows Charity likes you."

"I'm goin' back, but not you, Curly. It's all quicksand, and I'll never get out alive. No need you goin' down with me."

"We've been pardners for fifteen years, and I'm goin'."

Freddie stood up, and they got to their feet. "Well, I'm going too, so maybe the three of us can do something about all this injustice."

"You'd be puttin' yourself in danger," Bronco said.

"Oh, fiddle. I'm not afraid of any Sladek."

She walked up to the porch and turned smiling as the two men tipped their hats in awe.

Curly bowed. "Mighty glad to make your acquaintance, ma'am."

Bronco stood dazed, still shaken, but nodding.

She went back inside, and he sank down on the bench.

"I always figured the Sladeks done it."

"There's no evidence. Just talk from a dead man."

"You can go back, Curly. Watchin' Charity with the Sladeks will tear your heart out."

"But with Freddie here, there's hope."

"Yeah, someone to cry over our graves."

Traveling with Freddie was an education in itself, and Bronco and Curly enjoyed the trip with her.

It was of a morning when they came to the spot where the cattle had been bedded down, and late afternoon when the stage rolled into Bear Creek. It was a small town, around three hundred people, the driver had said, with no local law and no churches.

The valley spread green and wooded in all directions. Blue mountains lined the horizons in every direction but south.

Some twenty buildings were set along the wide street on either side with houses spread out behind them. A wooden bridge into town crossed a sweet water creek that was deep and rocky and ran east to west. The first building on the left was boarded up, but the rest were active. Boardwalks had been built.

There were four stores and one saloon, an

express office where the stage had pulled up, and a livery at the north end of town.

After helping Freddie get her luggage to a rooming house run by a Mrs. Bromley west of town and up a slope, Bronco and Curly went to the livery to put up their horses for the night. The skinny youth with a toothy grin was about seventeen and named Randy. He was running the livery and had no love for the Sladeks.

"They causes a lot of trouble."

"Sladeks got a big ranch, have they?" Curly asked,

"Half of this part of Montana. And they ain't bashful about it either. Folks ain't too happy the way they're bringin' in all that cattle. Sooner or later, they'll need more grass. And the other ranchers ain't givin' 'em any."

"That roomin' house the only place to stay?"

Randy took their measure. "Do you snore?"

"Not much," Curly said.

"I got a house all to myself. My pa died and left me the livery and a place out back. I take care of the stage horses, but it don't pay much. And I can use more money. Maybe five dollars a week? Each, I mean. I'll throw in the stalls."

"You got a deal," Curly said. "But we'll buy some of the chuck."

Randy grinned. "Okay."

They groomed their weary horses, then turned as a shadow from the front door spread across the straw and reached to their boots.

It was Lazlo.

EIGHT

"All right, Bronco, we saw you ridin' in."
The tall man looked ten feet high in the late afternoon sun, his shadow longer by the moment. His big hands were lifted at his sides, working his fingers.

Now there was another man with a rifle. Boney; leaning on the side of the barn door, watched. Randy started to offer his livery services, then realized there was trouble and backed away.

Lazlo came a few feet into the building, his face set in a sneer. "You've been lucky, Bronco. But now I'm gonna twist your head off like you was a chicken. And you, kid, get out of here. We don't want no witnesses."

Randy was angry. "This is my barn."

"Yeah, well, there's gonna be a couple dead

men in here. Stick around if you want to join 'em."

Curly rested his hand on his six-gun. "Go on, Randy."

"I ain't leavin'."

Bronco waved his hand toward him. "Get out, son."

Randy hesitated, then turned and went out the back door. Lazlo came a bit closer and slowly unbuckled his gunbelt, letting it fall.

"First I'm gonna beat you fair and square. Then I'm gonna blow your head off."

Bronco drew a deep breath, then unbuckled his gunbelt. He knew the big man meant every word, and there was no law in this town. Boney had the drop on them with a Winchester repeater.

Lazlo began to stalk Bronco, and they moved slowly in a wide circle, hands lifted, watching each other like roosters.

Suddenly, Lazlo charged, and Bronco danced aside. Lazlo stumbled against a post and turned around, eyes blazing. He charged again, and Bronco ducked, but the big man landed on him, and they grappled as Bronco fell into the stall, knocking his buckskin aside.

As the men rolled in the straw the buckskin

began to kick and snort. They rolled between its legs, and Lazlo was kicked in the shoulder. They fought their way out into the open, pounding each other as Lazlo tried to get a grip on him.

"Blast you, Bronco. You're like a worm."

They were gasping for air as they broke apart and sprang to their knees. Lazlo was getting ready to charge when suddenly Bronco charged him, head-first into his belly. Lazlo staggered back, the wind knocked out of him as he tried to get ahold of Bronco's ears. But Bronco squirmed free and landed a blow on the man's jaw.

Lazlo fell back, then roared like a bull and charged again. Bronco jumped aside and slammed his fist on the back of the man's head, then kicked him in the rear. Lazlo stumbled against the post, recovered, and turned around.

With a fierce roar, Lazlo rushed him, and Bronco was caught in the man's powerful grip. They struggled, and Bronco kicked him in the shins, breaking away. Lazlo stalked him again as Bronco backed toward the post.

When Lazlo put his head down and charged, Bronco stepped aside at the last second, and Lazlo crashed head-on into the post, his skull cracking with a pop and the post buckling.

The overhead loft, supported by the post, trembled.

Lazlo fell to his knees, shaking his head crazily. He saw his gunbelt close by and pretended to collapse with a moan. Then he grabbed his weapon and rolled over, firing at Bronco, who dodged and dived for his Colt.

Curly was still held by Boney's rifle.

Lazlo fired as Bronco rolled sideways, whipped up his Colt and fired at the same time as Lazlo's third shot. He hit Lazlo between the eyes. The big man was on his knees, startled and staring crazily. Bronco was on one knee, his back to Boney and breathing hard.

Boney straightened. "Drop it."

Bronco hesitated, weighing his chances of whirling around and firing in time. Lazlo fell face forward in the straw, sprawled and dead.

"No, you drop it," Randy said, his rifle barrel shoved into Boney's back. "Or I'll split you like a chunk of wood."

Slowly Boney lowered his weapon, and Randy reached around to grab the rifle and tuck it under his arm. Then Randy took the man's six-gun and emptied it, holstering it again.

"Now get that friend of yours out of my barn."

It wasn't easy for a skinny man like Boney to

drag Lazlo out of the barn, but he did. Out in the fading sunlight, three townspeople paused to help him throw the big man over the saddle. Randy emptied the rifle and returned it. He did the same with Lazlo's six-gun and hung the gunbelt over Lazlo's saddle horn.

When Boney was riding out of town Randy turned to look at a dozen men who had gathered out of curiosity.

"It was a fair fight," Randy said.

One of the men was sweating and wiping his brow.

"But he's a Sladek hand. We're in for it now."

Curly came forward. "Don't you fellas worry about it. This is a personal matter."

Reluctantly the men wandered away, and Curly came back inside, testing the post that was holding the loft.

Bronco was having trouble catching his breath, but he finally got to his feet. "Every time he hit me, he near killed me."

"Well, ole Boney's gonna head right out to tell Leo."

"Good," Bronco said. "We need to get this thing going."

"What thing?" Randy asked.

"You feed us, we'll tell you," Curly said. "You

likely saved Bronco from being backshot, so we owe it to you."

As twilight fell, Freddie and Charity had supper at the rooming house. Randy brought Curly and Bronco out back to his house.

And Boney was hightailing it for the ranch, a good eight hours away under a bright moon.

But at the ranch, Leo was walking toward the house in the same moonlight. He was dirty and sweating and annoyed with Charity for her delay in choosing.

Lucas was walking at his side. "I think Charity likes me the best."

"Ain't so. I got the jump on you." They paused short of the porch, and Leo turned to his younger brother. "I'd sure like to see that will."

"Pa says we get everything, and that Elva gets nothin'."

"But not while he's alive. And he could change it."

Lucas nodded. "Yeah, and she's been workin' her ways on him. But he said we'd get our third one of these days soon."

"He always says that. Now Hooper and his men, they'll do anything for money. We could make a fortune down at the mines. Take a couple hundred head, out of the north meadows now and then. He'd never even miss 'em."

Lucas swallowed hard. "Go against Pa?"

"What's he ever done for us? Makes us work like hired hands. Gives us peanuts."

Lucas shrugged. "But right now, the only thing on his mind is Charity. You and me, we got to figure out who's gonna get her. I sure don't want that Emmy Lou. She's a spoiled brat."

"I'm the oldest. I get Charity. Besides, you can handle Emmy Lou. Whup her some."

Lucas made a face. "She ain't bad lookin'."

"She and her ma are useless. Don't even cook for Pa. But Biscuits makes better food than any woman, I'll wager, and I'd just as soon he kept doin' the cookin' for us."

"I bet Charity can cook."

They went up on the porch and inside, finding their father sitting in front of the hearth. Elva was doing needlepoint and looked up sweetly.

"Why, you boys must be exhausted. I'll just leave you with your father."

She rose, turned, and went up the stairs.

Leo and his brother plunked down in chairs,

and Frank stretched out lazily. "You get the supplies?"

"Yeah, but them merchants ain't very friendly. And you want any barbed wire, you got to freight it up here."

"Town don't like us," Frank said. "But there ain't no law out here. No Texas Rangers askin' questions. Just a couple marshals we ain't never seen. It's a big country, and it's all ours."

"What about me and Lucas?" Leo asked.

"I told you. When I'm ready, you get a share. When I'm gone, you get it all."

"Can we see the will?" Leo asked.

Frank glared at him. "Just take my word for it."

While the men talked Elva hovered above in the shadows on the landing, making faces. She spun around and went into her daughter's room. Emmy Lou was brushing her hair and turned around.

Elva angrily told her about the will. "All to them. I married him for nothing."

"But maybe he'll change it."

"I don't think so. You may have to marry one of those boys or we won't get any money."

"Why don't we just leave?"

Elva sat on the bed with a thump. "I put

too much time in this. We've never had one so rich. So you marry Leo or Lucas, and we'll take care of Frank."

"I cringe to think of their hands on me."

"I've had to do it four times, so it's your turn."

Emmy Lou made a face in her hand mirror. "Well, I'm not getting any younger. I guess it's time. Maybe Lucas. He's not very smart."

"I'll keep working on Frank, but I've under estimated him. He's been lying to me."

"What about Charity?"

Back in town at Randy's house, Bronco lay in the dark with a full belly on a feather bed.

Curly was across the room on another soft bed, snoring softly. Randy was up reading in the other room. And Bronco lay staring at the pale light through the door. Fury had coursed through him when he had learned from Freddie that it had been Sladeks who had hanged his father, and all his pent-up anger and misery had come forth, driving him toward vengeance.

But where would he get proof, and what chance would he have against Sladek and all his men, with no law to back him up? He fell asleep, tossing and turning all night.

It was early afternoon of the next day when

the weary Curly and Bronco awakened to the smell of bacon and eggs. They were in heaven as Randy served them at the table. The house was big, clean, and sparsely furnished. But it had an iron stove with an oven and hot biscuits.

"Eggs," Curly said. "I can't believe it."

"Used to be they come by freight, packed in lard. Now there's the Hawkins farm west of town. If Sladek doesn't overrun it. They got pigs and chickens and milk cows."

As they ate, Bronco kept thinking of what he was going to do, and then Randy asked him the same question.

Bronco shrugged. "Maybe I don't have to do nothin'. They come after me once. They'll come again. We'll pick 'em off a few at a time. Sooner or later, the truth will come out."

"Yeah," Curly grunted, "if they don't get us first. What we need is some law around here."

"There's a Marshal Norton in this part of the territory, supposed to open an office here," Randy said. "We ain't never seen 'im, but they keep sayin' he's comin'. And there's an Army camp to the west, about a week's ride. Some second lieutenant and about thirty men."

"Maybe you oughta wait on Norton," Curly said.

"Sladek ain't waitin'."

There was a knock on the door, and a young girl about Randy's age was allowed inside, but the door remained open. She was blonde and perky and had pretty brown eyes. She wore an apron over her calico dress and looked excited.

"Sally Bromley, what are you doing here alone?" Randy demanded. "Your ma will whup you."

"I came to tell you. A man rode in from the Sladeks and said they're going to have a big picnic and dance next Saturday, right here in town. They'll bring a couple sides of beef. And they'll have bronc riding and a shooting match and games. They're paying for everything. Mr. Sladek's ward's come to town, and it's a celebration. Day after tomorrow."

Randy frowned, folding his arms. "I suppose folks are happy about that."

"We all are," she said, making a face. "Except you."

Randy introduced her to his guests, then pushed her on outside. "You go on home, Sally."

"Last time I ever bring you any news," she said.

"Go home, Sally."

She paused, smiling only for him. "I heard

how you helped out in that fight. Wasn't you afraid?"

"No, now get out of here."

He closed the door on her and turned around, pausing as he saw Curly and Bronco's grin. Then he blushed red.

"She's cute, huh."

Bronco leaned back in his chair. "So Sladek's comin' to town. When he finds out about Lazlo, he'll have somethin' else in mind."

"Right now, we need to get cleaned up," Curly said.

"You can use the horse trough and pump out behind the barn," Randy said. "And the general store has clothes you can buy."

So it was that Bronco shaved and they both bathed and bought new clothes, changing in the back room and feeling good. As they came into the front of the cluttered store toward evening, they both paused, staring through the hanging boots and harness and pickle barrels.

Freddie was at the counter, waiting.

"Mrs. Bromley's daughter told you about Saturday, I suppose. I've decided to surprise the Sladeks and not let them know I'm here until the celebration. They won't dare do anything to me then."

Curly looked Freddie over and then leaned on the counter near her. "You didn't hear about the fight?"

"Yes. What happened?"

"Lazlo got shot tryin' to kill Bronco here."

"Bronco, you really need a keeper. Now tell me, can you dance?"

He gazed at her in surprise. "No."

Freddie smiled at Curly. "And you?"

"Nope. Come on, Bronco, we got work to do."

Bronco hurried out the door with Curly on his heels, and they crossed over to the livery as fast as they could walk. Once inside the barn, they both sat down on the bales of straw near the entrance.

"Lord a' mighty," Curly said. "There's nothin' scarier than a good woman."

Bronco grinned. "Yeah, and that's a fact."

But they both sobered, and Curly pushed his hat back as he spat. "What are we gonna do, Bronco? I got a feelin' we're back so deep in quicksand, we'll never get out."

"I got to know who killed my father."

"Worries me that Freddie figured out who you are."

"She's a schoolteacher. Never could fool them."

"Well, if Leo didn't recognize us, maybe Frank won't."

"If he does, Curly, you'd better duck."

"I'll go down fightin' afore they ever get another noose around my neck."

"I reckon I feel the same. Right now, I think after I ride Trigger Foot, Sladek'll hire me. I can work on gettin' information from his men. And maybe you could spend more time with Freddie. She might remember somethin' else. Unless you're scared of her."

Curly shrugged and wiped his brow. "Man gets out of practice with women. And I just wasn't interested since my wife died. I tell you, Bronco, she was the prettiest thing you ever saw. Ole Frank used to drool whenever he saw her in town, and he was married at the time."

"That why he took your land?"

"It crossed my mind."

"Right now, he's puttin' on this big show to impress Charity."

"And look at me, Bronco. What kind of impression do I make, even cleaned up like this?"

"Trust me, Curly. There's no figurin' what a woman's going to do."

NINE

On Friday morning, Charity was wearing her riding outfit and surveying the gold silk dress that Elva had given her, and she didn't like it. It had flowers hanging all over it, and the neck was rather low. She sat in front of the dresser and clipped off the flowers. Then she took lace from a shawl and started sewing it over the neckline to raise it.

There was a knock on her door. She turned.

"Come in."

It was Frank with his coat on, smelling like he'd had a bath, but wearing his sidearm as usual. He pulled up a chair near her, pipe in the comer of his mouth.

"That's a pretty dress."

"It is now. I'll wear it to the dance."

"I want you to be so pretty you'll knock their

boots off. I want this town at your feet."

She smiled. "That's a big order."

"You can do it, Charity."

"What about Emmy Lou?"

"Never mind about her. It's you that's gonna be the princess around here. Anything you want, you just holler."

"I need more clothes. Most of them were lost."

"You get anything you want, Charity."

"Thank you, Uncle Frank."

"Have you forgotten about that Bronco fellow?"

She avoided his gaze and nodded, but he knew she was covering up, and it angered him. Yet he brushed it off and stood up slowly.

"Well, he's gone, Charity, so it don't matter. Besides, either one of my two boys would make a good husband."

"Yes, I know."

"Now, you need anything, you let me know."

He gave her a kiss on the cheek and left the room. Minutes later, there was another knock. Emmy Lou came swaying inside, all dressed up and primping her hair as she came over. "Frank is finally going to hire a housekeeper for us. A woman from town."

"Why do we need a housekeeper?"

"Oh, Charity, you're so naive."

Charity ignored her and continued sewing on the lace while Emmy Lou sat on the bed and kept fussing with her clothes.

"You know, Charity, one of us has to marry Leo and one has to marry Lucas. Which one do you want?"

"I don't care."

"I'll take Lucas. He has a cute smile."

"I'm in no hurry."

"Oh, but Frank wants a double wedding soon."

Charity set the dress down. "I don't care what he wants. I'm not ready."

Emmy Lou laughed. "Oh, you have a temper. Shame on you. Leo will beat you for that."

Charity turned, her voice icy. "Don't you have something else to do?"

"Oh, my, no. There's absolutely nothing to do here."

"You could cook, or dust, or sweep."

Emmy Lou got to her feet. "I'm trying to be friendly. Well, you just sit there and be nasty."

The young woman left the room in a huff, and Charity leaned back in her chair, shaking her head and fighting her tears. Curly and

Bronco had left for good, and she wasn't sure why it upset her so much.

She heard commotion outside her window, and she stood up, sliding up the pane so she could hear better. Down below, Boney was riding up with a body across the saddle of another horse. It was Lazlo, long arms dangling.

Charity leaned half out the window, listening.

Frank Sladek was on the porch, hands on his hips.

Leo and Lucas came running up from the corrals.

"Now what happened?" Frank demanded.

Boney reined up and pushed his hat back, wiping his brow. "We saw Bronco and Curly in town. Lazlo went after him."

"And Bronco killed him?"

"Dead."

"I thought those two left a long time ago."

"They come back."

"I wonder why."

Charity drew back, elated, but she kept listening, making sure they could not see her. Her face was burning, her hands damp as she gripped the curtains.

"What do you want to do?" Boney asked.

"Bury Lazlo. What else?"

Frank went back inside, and Boney led the horse with the body away. But Leo and Lucas stood grim just below her window.

"What now?" Lucas asked.

"I'm gonna talk to Cord."

As they walked away, Charity drew a deep breath. She slid the window closed as quietly as possible, and she sat down, smiling to herself. Then she went back to fixing the dress. But her frown returned as she wondered why Leo wanted to speak with Cord.

Bronco and Curly, back in town. It made her happy, flustered, and fearful all at the same time. And the celebration was tomorrow. Could Bronco stay on Trigger Foot?

Bronco was wondering the same thing as he and Curly had supper with Freddie at the rooming house. Mrs. Bromley was large and round and rosy with a little nose and a big laugh. The food was delicious. The rooms were all pretty with lace curtains and big soft pillows on the leather furniture. The dining room had a big table under a small crystal chandelier.

Sally was sitting next to Freddie and looked across the table. "Are you still staying at Randy's?"

"Sure am," Curly said.

"He's bashful," Sally said, blushing. "He'd better be dancing with me."

"If he don't, I will," Curly replied.

"You don't know how," Freddie said. "I'd better teach you. Mrs. Bromley, can you still play that spinet?"

The woman allowed as how she could, and they all went into the parlor where the small, upright piano sat in the comer away from the fireplace. Curly and Bronco were reluctant, but both Sally and Freddie took them in hand.

Learning to dance with Freddie was an experience for Curly, his heart drumming all over his chest. Both men stepped all over their feet, but by evening's end, they at least could move around the floor.

Curly liked holding Freddie, and she knew it. Once he stumbled, and they ended up clutching each other. Her eyes twinkled.

"If you ever shave off that beard, I might even marry you."

Curly grinned and held her a little tighter, but she pulled away with a smile. The dance lessons continued.

When they all sat down, weary and out of breath, Mrs. Bromley brought in the coffee.

Later, walking down the slope in the starlight, Curly shook his head.

"Man, that was somethin'. Us dancin'."

"I saw all that goin' on between you and Freddie."

"Man, she is something. When I get ahold of her at the dance, I'm gettin' me a kiss."

"Well, I ain't sure I'll be doin' any dancin' after I get on old Trigger Foot tomorrow."

They slept well that night, and in the morning they looked out the window to see the excitement in town. Across from the livery and behind the express office, tables were being set up and a barbecue pit dug and surrounded with rocks, the sides of beef already turning. Randy was skeptical.

"They're all happy because the Sladeks are payin' for everything and puttin' up prize money."

"What about you?" Curly asked.

"Sladeks are tryin' to buy the town, and I don't like it."

But the whole town seemed to love it. As morning drew long, under a bright sunny sky, the three hundred townspeople, along with ranchers and cowboys, farmers and drifters, all were gathering at the picnic site. Women wore their frillies and bonnets, men were hauling food, and children ran around in circles.

Games were already going on, especially the three-legged race where men's legs were tied together.

While Curly helped Freddie with some pies she had baked, Bronco wandered through the crowd, waiting for the Sladeks to show. He was nervous about seeing Charity again, uneasy about riding the famed Trigger Foot, and furious with the Sladeks, but he didn't know how to learn the truth.

Then he paused to watch five cowhands coming into town. They had ropes from their saddles to the neck of a very tall, big-shouldered, snorting, kicking, bucking animal the likes of which Bronco had never seen. Trigger Foot was a blue roan, with unusually long legs and muscles bulging in his neck and shoulders. He had a large head and bulging eyes. The riders kept their distance, stretching him between them.

Bronco watched them as they took him to the empty round corral in back of the livery. When they were out of sight, he wiped his brow with his bandanna.

Curly had come over with a grin. "Well, now."

"That's the biggest horse I ever seen," Bronco said. "It's a mighty long fall from that one."

Bronco straightened. "I'll ride 'im."

"Five dollars you can't," said a merchant, who had been listening.

"I'd better warn you," said Curly. "This is Bronco Wade."

"Never heard of him. You want my five or not?"

"You're covered."

And so the betting started. But first there were more games and horse races. And there was food, plenty of it—beef turning on the rods over a hot fire, pies and cakes and salads and everything else to turn a man's appetite.

Soon, more Sladek riders were coming in, Hooper and Krinkle and Boney in front. It was Krinkle who rode over to Bronco and Curly, leaning on the pommel and grinning, his handlebar mustache moving up and down.

"Well, now, I saw what you did to Lazlo."

"He asked for it," Bronco said.

"They want you dead. Leo thinks you got some hold on Charity."

"That the only reason?"

"You got another?" Krinkle asked.

"Not so far."

"I guess you've seen Trigger Foot."

Bronco nodded. "He's a big one."

"And mean as a mother bear."

Krinkle chuckled and turned his horse about, riding to the livery. Bronco swallowed and looked at the grinning Curly, who was still taking bets. Krinkle returned to put some money on Bronco.

Now Bronco saw the Sladek buggies coming toward town, two of them. In the front was a hefty, round-faced woman in a blue dress with a white bonnet. Next to her was a perky young woman in yellow. They were being driven by Lucas.

"That's Lucas," Krinkle said. "And Sladek's wife and stepdaughter, Emmy Lou."

The second buggy was being driven by Leo with Charity at his side. She was wearing a gingham dress in blue and white and looking gorgeous. Bronco drew a deep breath when he saw her. If only his life wasn't ruled by memories and anger and frustration, if only...

"And that's Frank Sladek," Krinkle said.

Curly stopped taking bets. Bronco started to sweat.

Frank Sladek was a good-sized man with big, rough features and a pipe in the comer of his wide mouth. He had heavy shoulders and wore a cowhide vest over a new blue shirt. His dark eyes scanned the crowd. Riding next to him was Tom Tyree and his brother.

When the Tyrees saw Bronco, they let out a yell and dug in their heels, riding at a lope to pass the buggies and skid to a halt near the picnic tables, raising dust so that the women turned and called them names.

Tom jumped down and grabbed their hands. "Wow, you're back. Are we glad to see you."

Billy came to join them, grinning broadly. "We heard what you done to Lazlo."

"It was a fair fight," Curly said.

Bronco turned to see Charity twisting in the buggy, trying to get a look at him. He raised his hand slightly. She waved, and Leo cracked the whip on the team to get it turned to the livery.

Frank Sladek gave up his horse to one of his hands and came walking over. Bronco and Curly nearly wet their britches as he approached, but he didn't recognize them one bit. Bronco glanced at Curly, who was as shaken as he was, but they stood quiet as Torn Tyree introduced them.

"Well, Bronco Wade, is it?" Frank mused.

"I thought you was a lot bigger than you are, after what you done to Lazlo."

"I'm big enough."

"You get a look at Trigger Foot?"

"Sure did."

"The prize money is five hundred."

Bronco moistened his lips. "This may be the time you got to pay off."

Frank grinned. "Well, now, we'll see about that.

What about you, Curly? You want to give it a try?"

"Nope."

Frank laughed and wandered off, and Bronco wiped his face with the back of his hand. He looked at Curly, who had been holding his breath and now was trying to relax. The Tyrees saw young Sally and took off after her, and Krinkle headed for the beef.

Bronco and Curly stood alone, listening to the fiddlers start up some lively tunes, and they looked at each other.

"Curly, I near died when Frank looked at us."

"Thank the Lord, we're okay."

"Not a sign of recognition."

"So now what?"

"When I ride that horse, he'll offer us a job,

and we can name the price."

Curly shrugged. "I ain't pressin' my luck. I'll hold the fort in town."

"Wait'll he sees Freddie."

As people gathered for the food, Bronco looked for Charity, but Leo had her secluded somewhere in the crowd. As Freddie came toward Curly, Charity suddenly squealed from behind a group of people and came running out.

"Freddie!"

"Charity."

The two women hurried to each other, hugging and kissing while everyone stared. Including Leo and Lucas. When Frank came back to see what was going on, he was surprised and appeared angry.

"What the devil are you doing here?"

Freddie smiled, her arm around Charity. "Now, now, Frank. You want to be a hero to this town, you don't yell at women. You have to be a gentleman."

"Nobody said you was comin'."

"Didn't you get Nora's letter?"

"Never got no letter."

"That's nice."

Frank spun on his heel and nearly crashed

into Elva, who insisted on being introduced. It took all of Frank's control to get through that phase, and then he stormed off.

"You mustn't mind Frank," Elva said. "He's easily upset."

Freddie looked her over. "Is that so?"

"I do have to keep after him to relax."

"I thought he was easily bored."

Elva had to think about that for a moment, trying to decide if she was being insulted, and Freddie smiled, turning to Charity, who was leading her over toward Bronco and Curly.

"Freddie, I want you to meet my best friends."

"I've met them, dear."

"Bronco saved my life. And Curly looked after me."

"Well, I'm here now."

"Aren't you taking a terrible chance?" Charity asked softly.

"I'll not have you marrying anyone on my account."

"But if Frank finds out—"

"I don't care if he does or not."

"Shhh."

Freddie put her arm around her. "Charity, you forget, I'm not afraid of anyone."

Before they could join Curly and Bronco,

the shooting match began. Leo and Lucas were matching shot for shot with Bronco with Winchesters, and it was Bronco who kept winning. Leo and Bronco were tied for the fifty-dollar prize. The target was moved another twenty feet away. The crowd held its breath, and Leo missed the mark.

But Bronco got down on one knee, aimed, and fired, hitting the mark dead center.

"You're just lucky," Leo growled, eyes blazing.

There was a fast-draw contest, but Cord never appeared for it. Two dozen men took turns whipping out a six-gun to try to hit a bull's-eye in the target. Curly had pushed Bronco into that contest as well, and some men whistled when Bronco whipped up his six-gun so fast no one saw his hand move.

In the end, it was Bronco who won the fifty dollars. Leo and Lucas cast dirty glances his way as Bronco took his prize. Bronco looked around for Charity and Freddie, and he saw them walking over with Curly.

Then the crowd fell silent as Frank Sladek stood up on a box, and everyone clapped. "We got us this horse that's never been rode. Now who wants to earn five hundred dollars? We pay all funeral expenses if you lose."

There was laughter, and most of the men wandered over to the livery to have a look at the big horse, which was kicking and bucking and spinning. Some of the women followed at a distance.

Freddie and Charity stood on the boardwalk by the express office with Bronco and Curly, watching the crowd moving across the street.

Bronco paused and looked at Curly, who was grinning and trying to appear confident Bronco wouldn't get thrown all the way to Texas.

"Five hundred dollars," Curly said. "They must not expect to pay off."

"Seems like."

"Bronco, you'll get hurt," Charity said. "That horse breaks all the corral fences. He chases anyone that comes near."

Bronco acted nonchalant, but as he crossed the wide street his knees were watery and buckling.

TEN

Trigger Foot was snorting and pawing the earth. The roan was so tall it could have walked over the fence, but it chose to parade around, tossing its big head and kicking up its heels. Men crowded the railings, shaking their heads in awe.

"Man," a merchant said, "he sure looks mean."

Randy got close to the fence, Sally at his elbow. "Aw, he ain't that bad."

"You gonna ride 'im?" the merchant asked.

"Nah, because when Bronco gets through, he'll be broke."

Bets were being passed around, and Curly kept telling everyone up front that Bronco had never been thrown by a bronc. No one believed him, and some laughed.

Suddenly, the roan kicked up its heels,

knocked two middle boards out of the fence and threw six men flying in all directions. The men crashed into the crowd and knocked others down, and some were cursing. For a moment, everyone stared, and then they began to laugh.

Bronco wasn't laughing. He knew he'd met his match.

It took six men with ropes and a blindfold to put on the double-rigged Texas saddle that had seen better days. Dust rose so thick in the struggle that no one could see what was happening for about ten minutes. When the dust settled, the six men had ropes around Trigger Foot's neck pulled in two directions.

The roan stood still, nostrils flaring under the blindfold, ears back and legs spread out, only a halter with a single rope on its head.

Frank was in the saddle outside the fence but sitting above the crowd for effect. "Now then, folks, you see before you the meanest horse ever lived. Who's gonna be first?"

"Bronco," Tom shouted. "Bronco Wade."

Curly muttered. "Bronco, you should let someone else tire him out."

"No, if I want that job, I got to make a show."

Bronco climbed up on the top rail and looked around, seeing Leo and Lucas riding up next to Frank, and there was Cord, up in the wide opening of the barn loft with Hooper, Boney, and a dozen other men, watching and waiting.

Another rider, a stranger on a black horse with bedroll and large saddlebags, appeared behind Frank and his sons, a tall, slim man with wide shoulders, black leather vest, heavy leather coat, and black hat with turned-down brim. He had a hard, square face and wasn't smiling.

Bronco looked for Charity, but he couldn't see her. It was just as well, he thought. He didn't want her to see him mashed to a pulp.

"The first rider," Frank shouted, "is Bronco Wade. Now, folks, I hear he has a reputation from down in Wyoming as a feller that's never been throwed. Well, today's the day his record is broken. But we play fair, folks. We got the stirrups set to his long legs already."

The crowd was getting so excited it crowded the fences, even knowing it could be dangerous.

Curly climbed up beside Bronco. "You sure about this?"

"You stay back. There's enough fellers out there to get me on board."

Bronco removed his coat and handed it to Curly. He pulled his hat down tight, felt sweat forming under his clothes, and dropped down into the corral.

Trigger Foot stood perfectly still while Bronco went around to the left side and paused, then reached for the rope and horn, sliding his boot into the stirrup. His heart was going wild in his chest, and his ice blue eyes were round with dread.

"Folks," Frank called out. "I'd get away from the fence if I was you."

Some of the men tried to fall back, but the crowd was pushing forward behind them. Tom and Billy Tyree climbed onto a top rail just the same, one leg on each side so they could jump off quick, but they would have to land on top of everyone else.

"Go get 'em, Bronco," Tom shouted.

Bronco's boot was in the stirrup. His left hand held the rope and horn, and he drew a deep breath. It was sure a long way up. Suddenly, he was reaching for the saddle, throwing his right leg over and finding the stirrup. Sladek was right. It was a fit. He pulled his hat down tight.

Between his legs was so much power, he swallowed hard.

He could see nothing now beyond the laid–

back ears and the thin, scrawny neck with a mangy streak of hair dangling. Slowly he took his left hand from the horn, switched the halter rope to his right hand, and put his left arm in the air.

Bronco was sore afraid, but he nodded to the rope holders. They came as close as they dared to take the ropes off the long neck of Trigger Foot, and one brave fellow pulled off the blindfold. Then they scrambled for the fence and dived over it.

"Let 'er rip!" someone shouted.

But Trigger Foot stood still a long moment.

Bronco tried not to hold his breath, but he was plenty scared. He tried to act brave and nonchalant, waving his left hand high.

Then the roan put its head down, ears still back. Its rear end shot straight up, nearly pitching Bronco straight out of the saddle. It went forward like a hurricane, spun like a tornado, grunting and blowing air and kicking and bucking, hardly touching the ground.

Bronco sat the saddle in terror, but he kept his legs tight and held to the rope in silent prayer. He couldn't see the crowd, only the dust rising furiously around him.

Every time Trigger Foot went into the air,

it seemed he went higher, and when he came down, Bronco felt a body jar so hard, his ears seemed to slide into his hat and his boots up to his chin.

Yet Bronco stayed, and the furious roan spun and jumped and whirled around, pitching and flying high while the crowd cheered.

Bronco's body was so shattered, he didn't feel the pain.

Seconds went by, then minutes.

"Look out," someone shouted.

The roan slammed against the fence, trying to knock him off, scattering the crowd. Bronco was sure his right leg was broken, but he stayed on, and the roan kicked some more.

Then the roan went into a spin, round and round and round, trying to whirl Bronco off. Bucking and spinning, head down, until Bronco was so dizzy he nearly reached for the horn, but he kept his hands free.

Panting and sweating, Trigger Foot went into a sudden gallop around the corral, kicking and bucking every few yards, but Bronco stayed in the saddle. Minutes passed, and Bronco was sure every bone in his body was broken.

The roan slammed his other leg against the fence, reared up, sending the Tyrees sailing into the crowd, and spun again. Then it came to such a sudden halt, Bronco almost went over his head, but settled back in the saddle.

Trigger Foot reared up on hind legs and started to go over backward. Frantic, Bronco jerked the halter rope, twisting the roan's head around to the side, forcing it to drop back down.

It was a full twenty minutes before the roan came to a halt and stood trembling, panting for air, shaking its head.

The crowd was roaring. Bronco prayed it was over.

But Trigger Foot was only getting another breath. Then the roan started bucking again. This time, however, it lasted only a few minutes, and the roan was just too plumb tired.

"It's over, folks," Frank shouted.

Bronco reined the roan next to the fence where the Tyrees reached for him, and he left the saddle and let them pull him up on the top rail. His body felt broken for sure.

"Lord a'mighty," Billy said happily.

"Are your legs broke?" Tom asked. "Thought they was, but no."

The crowd reached up and grabbed Bronco off the fence, setting him on the shoulders of two merchants and dancing him around with glee.

Frank Sladek rode through the crowd to rein up next to Bronco, looking him directly in the eye. "Son, you just won five hundred dollars. And a job if you want it. I've never seen a man could ride like that. How about it?"

"I'll let you know," Bronco said, coming back to life.

The merchants carried Bronco across the street to the picnic tables and shoved drinks and food at him. They were slapping him on the back because, even though Sladeks were paying for everything, they had no love for them. Seeing Bronco best Trigger Foot had made them so tickled, they couldn't stop laughing and cheering.

Curly made his way over to shake Bronco's hand and return his coat. "We won two hundred on you. How do you feel?"

"Like I was rolled on. I need to clean up again."

As the crowd fell away to eat and drink some more, Randy came with Sally trailing, congratulating him before wandering off with the girl on his arm. The Tyrees had to come and express their glee another time. Leo and Lucas and the Sladek hands avoided him, except for Krinkle.

The burly man shook his hand. "I don't for the life of me know how you stayed up there, Bronco, but you ever need a friend, you got it."

"Thanks."

Krinkle wandered off, and abruptly Charity and Freddie were there with Bronco and Curly. Freddie came and kissed him on the cheek.

"Bronco, I never thought you'd amount to anything, but seeing you beat Frank Sladek has made my day. Now, Curly, you and I are going over to have some of that dessert."

Curly didn't resist as the woman led him away.

Charity was alone with Bronco, and she took his big hand in both of hers. She was aglow with pleasure, her red hair glistening in the sunlight, eyes shining.

"I'm so proud of you, Bronco."

"I'm all crippled up again."

"Too crippled to dance with me tonight?"

He shook his head. "Nope."

"Of course," she said with a laugh, "you've already done a lot of dancing. The way you were riding air, it was really a sight to see."

"Didn't feel like no air under me."

"Uncle Frank was really impressed."

She stood on her tiptoes and kissed his cheek

as he bent his head, then she turned around right into Leo, who had hurried over. Leo grabbed her arm.

"Come on, Charity."

She frowned but walked with him into the crowd.

Bronco drew a deep breath, wondering if he could ever put away his misery long enough to think just how he felt about her.

He turned to reach for some lemonade but paused.

Standing on the other side of the table was the stranger with the hard, square face and heavy leather coat over his black vest. His black hat with the turned-down brim made him look sinister. His blue eyes were as icy as Bronco's.

"Bronco Wade?"

"Who wants to know?"

The man lifted his coat from his left vest, revealing a circled star in the center of a silver badge. "I'm a deputy U.S. marshal. Let's have a talk."

ELEVEN

B ronco's throat went dry as he stared at the
man's badge gleaming in the sunlight. Jim
Hodges and Wiley Haines had been hunted in
Texas, thanks to the Sladeks, and that thought
made him mighty nervous.

He nodded and walked around the tables,
then followed the tall man back through the
happy crowd over to the express office, walking
around in front, standing in the shade on the
boardwalk and listening to the roar of the
crowd behind the building.

"I'm Phil Norton."

Bronco leaned on the post, folding his arms,
trying to act casual. "You passin' through?"

"Going to open an office here."

"They can use it."

"Heard you won the shootin' contest."

"It was close," Bronco said.

"And I saw you ride that bronc. Man can ride like that, he has to be an honest man." The lawman stood with feet apart, thumbs in his gunbelt. "I need an honest man to wear a badge in this part of the territory."

Bronco's heart stopped, then went loco. "A badge?"

"Ever wear one?"

"No, I spent the last fifteen years on broncs."

"And before that?"

Bronco shrugged, taking a crazy chance. "Could be I'm wanted for somethin' I didn't do. Somethin' that happened when I was a fifteen-year-old kid. Down in Texas."

"Maybe I could straighten it out."

"I was figurin' on workin' for Sladek."

"Why?"

Uneasy, Bronco stared into the street. "He's the one got me in trouble. I think he murdered my father. But I can't prove it. I was lookin' to find some proof out there."

Norton studied him a long moment. "You could help yourself a lot better with a badge."

Curly came around the comer. "Hey, Bronco, I—"

"Curly, this here's Phil Norton, deputy U.S.

marshal."

His mouth open, Curly just stared.

"He wants me to wear a badge."

"You?"

"Says maybe he can straighten out Texas for me. Could be, he can help you too."

"Nothin' can help us with Texas."

Norton pushed his hat back. "I'd sure give it a try."

"You'd be buckin' the Sladeks," Curly said. "Everybody does that ends up dead or wanted."

"You want it to stay that way?" Norton asked.

"Blazes, no," Curly said.

"Why don't we have ourselves a talk?"

Bronco and Curly stared at each other, and Bronco tugged at his hat. "I'm sore all over, Curly, and I'm sick and tired of bein' stomped on by broncs and earnin' my livin' that way. We've been savin' our money, but what good's it gonna do us if we got Texas hangin' over our heads?"

Curly wiped his mouth with the back of his hand. "Well, marshal, we'd be takin' a big chance on you."

"Just tell me the truth, and we'll see."

Both men gazed at the marshal for a long time, but Norton appeared solid, trustworthy, and blatantly honest. They took his measure and glanced at each other, both nodding.

As the afternoon shadows grew long, Curly told their story right out, clear and with detail that made him touch the bum still on his throat. Bronco told of his father's death over the water rights. Curly even told him about Charity.

"But she's not to know about me," Curly said. "I just don't want her hurt."

"Seems to me," the lawman said, "If any charges ever were filed, and I tell your story, I can get them dropped through our office in Texas. I'm sure the Rangers would cooperate."

Bronco stared at him. "Can't be that easy."

"I think it is," Norton said. "The carpetbaggers caused a lot of trouble down there after the war, and a few men like Sladek took advantage of the situation. I'll work on it. But right now, I could use a deputy here. I need honest men. And Bronco, you've got the job if you want it. Forty a month. And you can hire Curly for thirty."

Bronco turned to the bench and sat down, and Curly followed, both exhausted. They couldn't believe this was happening.

"I told you," Curly said. "The Good Lord

had somethin' in mind that we hadn't planned for. And this has got to be it. And I ain't goin' against Him."

"Me, neither," Bronco said."All right, Marshal."

Norton didn't seem to know how to smile, but his wide lips turned up at the corners. "I saw a boarded-up building at the entrance to town, near the bridge. We'll buy it and set you up. Agreed?"

"Sure thing," Bronco said.

They both stood as Norton held up his right hand. "Now hold up your hands and repeat after me: I solemnly swear to uphold the laws of this territory and the United States government, so help me God."

Bronco and Curly coughed in unison, then held up their hands and repeated the words. To their utter amazement, Norton was pinning badges on their vests, underneath their coats.

It was near twilight, and they heard the music.

"All right, boys, we'll finish this in the morning.

I'll camp outside of town and ride in at sunup. Meet you at that place by the bridge. For tonight, I'd hide those badges."

"Thanks, Marshal," Bronco said, "but we can

fix you up with a bunk at that white house back of the livery. Belongs to a kid named Randy, and I'm sure he'll agree. Door's open. You go on ahead, and we'll make it right."

Surprised, Norton nodded. "Thanks."

They stood up and shook his hands. Then the lawman crossed the street to his black horse and led it into the livery barn. Curly pulled off his hat and stroked his near bald head.

"Pinch me, Bronco."

"We come up here expectin' to die, and the next minute, I tell you, Curly, I ain't forgettin' my prayers no more."

"Me neither."

The music grew louder, and Curly removed his badge and pinned it on the underside of his vest, out of sight. Bronco did the same.

"Now what?" Curly asked.

"I think we try to get the goods on the Sladeks."

"Yeah, even if Frank figures out who we are, what's he gonna do to a couple deputy U.S. marshals?"

While the two men talked about the strange turn of events in their lives, Frank was having an argument with Charity away from the crowd under cover of the loud fiddle music. She was wearing the gold dress and looking fabulous, but Frank was plenty annoyed.

"You're out of your mind, Charity."

"But I like Bronco."

"He's a nothing. A saddle tramp. Ridin' Trigger Foot don't change that."

"He saved my life."

"That's no reason to stall my boys."

"But Uncle Frank—"

"Don't Uncle Frank me. You're just like your mother, goin' after the wrong…"

He caught his breath and turned red. Charity stared at him. Frank turned his back, trying to figure a way to cover up what he had said.

"Uncle Frank!"

"Go dance, Charity."

"What did you mean?"

"I didn't mean nothin'."

"You knew my mother? Tell me."

She grabbed his arm and spun him around, but he was furious now. "Charity, I'm gonna whup you if you don't get over there to Leo and Lucas. Nobody wanted you but me. Your folks threw you away like a dead chicken."

"But who were they?"

"You don't need to know. All you have to understand is they didn't want you, and I did.

Now get."

"But Uncle Frank—"

"Get!"

She backed away from his anger, tears filling her eyes, and she turned, but he caught her arm, stopping her.

"Charity, honey, I'm sorry. You're all that counts with me. Not my sons, not Elva or her silly daughter. Just you, Charity."

Tears trickled down her face. "But why won't you tell me?"

"Because it don't matter. Your folks are dead. A long time ago."

She trembled, and he turned her into his arms. She pressed her face to his chest, hugging him back. Then he released her.

"Now, honey, you go on and dance."

She smiled at him, wiping her eyes. "But I want to dance with you, Uncle Frank."

He drew the back of his hand across his own eyes."All right, honey. You know, I really wish you were my own daughter."

"I know."

"But blood ain't everything, Charity. As far as I'm concerned, you *are* my daughter, and that's the way it's gonna be. Now come on. Let's dance."

While Charity swayed on the board dance floor with Frank, Elva and Emmy Lou watched angrily from a distance. "He does anything she wants," Emmy Lou complained. "She's little goody two shoes."

"Don't worry, darling. We always win."

And they both smiled sweetly as townsmen asked them to dance. Meanwhile, Sally was chasing Randy, and the Tyree brothers were chasing Sally.

Freddie was fending off a couple of merchants when Curly appeared at her side. "Miss Freddie, this is our dance."

She was surprised as he whirled her away to the dance floor. "Why, Curly, what's come over you?"

"I'll tell you tomorrow. Right now, I'm gonna have the time of my life."

She laughed, and Curly swung her around as if he had danced all his life. He was stronger, bolder, his secret giving him confidence and new self-esteem.

Bronco too felt the change in himself. As stiff and sore as he was, barely able to walk, he started looking for Charity but paused, seeing her in Frank's arms.

Emmy Lou was at his side, slipping her

hand into his. "I'm Emmy Lou, Frank Sladek's stepdaughter. It would be good for you to dance with me. Frank would like you for it."

Bronco hesitated. She was no Charity, but he was feeling mighty good about himself, so he danced with her, and she fawned all over him.

As the song ended, Charity dragged Frank over. "It's time to switch partners, Emmy Lou."

"I don't want to."

Charity took her by the wrist, twisting it until Emmy Lou gasped, and she shoved her toward Frank, who caught her in surprise. Emmy Lou gave her a dirty look as she rubbed her wrist.

"You're awful mean, Charity."

Charity smiled. "Don't forget it."

And she turned into Bronco's startled arms. He held her as they danced into the crowd, staring into her lovely face.

"That's some dress," he said.

"Do you like it?"

"A bit low in front."

"It's the fashion."

"It's too low."

"You're jealous because other men like it."

"Am not."

"Am too."

And she laughed softly. They swung about,

and she was so light on her feet, it made him a better dancer. All the while, he was thinking how he might be free of the past, might even get his name back, might even…

She gazed up at him with a smile so sweet, he had a lump in his throat he couldn't swallow. When the dance ended, Leo came charging over to claim her.

Bronco watched him whirl her away into the next dance, but he was feeling pretty good about now. Emmy Lou had stepped on Charity's toes. Leo was bound to do the same.

He grinned to himself and left the dance floor, moving out through the crowd for some fresh air. And there, standing in the distance near the street, was Cord. He was just this side of the boardwalk, standing alone in the moonlight.

The sleazy gunfighter had his legs apart and was smiling. Bronco thought of the badge inside his vest, and he hesitated.

TWELVE

Cord hooked his thumbs in his gunbelt, the moonlight playing on the silver inlay. He had his hat pushed back, his dark eyes blazing, a twist to his crooked jaw.

Bronco walked slowly toward the man, music blaring behind him, and they both moved to place the dance out of the line of fire. They stopped some twenty feet apart.

"Bronco, I saw you in the fast draw. I can beat you real easy."

"That so?"

It was then that Krinkle came out of the crowd and hurried over, walking in front of Bronco, his back to Cord.

"Hey, Bronco, we got a game goin'. Come on."

Cord grimaced. "Get out of the way, Krinkle."

The burly man didn't even turn, taking Bronco by the shoulder. "You don't want to fight Cord," he muttered.

"I ain't turnin' tail."

"It's a fix."

"What do you mean?"

"If you win, there's a couple guns waitin' out there to finish you off and blame Cord."

"Leo's idea?"

"I ain't sayin'. I ride for the brand, remember? But you're my friend, Bronco, and I ain't lettin' you get wasted away for the likes of them. Besides, we need another hand at poker."

"Thanks, Krinkle, but I ain't runnin'."

"Then I got to cover you."

And Krinkle walked off into the shadows behind the express office. Bronco turned around and walked back far enough to make the spread just twenty feet.

Cord smiled, spreading his feet farther apart. "You first, Bronco."

"I'm not drawing on you, Cord."

"Well now, let's see what we can do to change your mind." And Cord reached into his pocket, drawing out a silver coin. "When this hits the ground, you'd better draw, or I'm pluggin' you."

Bronco felt damp all over and cold at the same time.

He'd never had a straight-out gunfight like this, and he wasn't anxious to see if his fast draw was going to be fast enough. Fun times on the cattle trail was one thing. But Cord was a professional. This was serious business. One or both of them was going to die. Sweat covered him, and his stomach reeled.

Suddenly, the music stopped between dances. He heard shouts, heard running feet that came to a halt at a safe distance to the side. From the comer of his eye, he could see that men had gathered.

Cord's sleazy smile widened. With a flick of his hand, the silver coin was tossed up into the moonlight.

As it danced in the air, Bronco was conscious of the chill of the night and the ice in his veins.

The coin sailed downward, and as it hit the dirt, Cord drew, but Bronco was faster, firing so fast Cord couldn't pull the trigger, hitting Cord dead center.

In the hush from the crowd, the shots echoed.

Cord doubled up in dismay, eyes wild. He staggered forward, dropping to his knees, trying to fire, then falling like a sack of grain, facedown, dead before he hit the dirt.

Bronco stood with his weapon in his hand, stunned by the action, ready to vomit. Krinkle came walking out of the shadows, and he moved close, speaking low.

"I put 'em to sleep. They don't even know it was me."

Bronco swallowed. "Now what?"

"Go have your dance."

"Thanks, Krinkle."

"You're the fastest gun I've ever seen."

Bronco holstered his Colt and wiped his brow with the back of his hand, then turned to see men coming toward them. Hooper and Boney were in the lead.

Randy came forward. "Wow, Bronco. You sure beat him all right. Me and Sally both saw it."

Frank Sladek was standing there with his sons, and Leo shook his head, then walked away. Lucas scowled, then followed his brother. The women had stayed back, but Bronco didn't feel like dancing anymore.

Curly came to his side. "Bronco, you sure took a chance."

They stood back as two men carried Cord's body away. Then Bronco, sick to his stomach, turned to the youth.

"Randy, I rented out that other bunk in your house."

"Huh?"

"I'll explain later. You comin', Curly?"

"I'm still dancin' with Freddie. I'll be along."

Bronco walked through the crowd and down to the street, then crossed over into the livery. His buckskin tossed its head, and he paused to stroke it.

"Hey, Bucky, did you see me ride that bronc?"

The buckskin snorted, and Bronco grinned, but then, as he turned away, he sobered. He didn't like killing a man, for whatever reason. He went on outside and over to the house. There was a lamp burning inside on the kitchen table, and he found Norton writing a long letter.

"My report," he said. "And letters to Texas."

Bronco poured himself a cup of coffee and sat down. "You really think you can clear it up?"

"You work for me now. I'll take care of it."

Bronco told him about Cord and how Krinkle helped.

Norton nodded. "I heard of Cord. I'm surprised you beat him. But your badge will be more respected now."

"Doesn't help my gut any."

"You'll be all right. I suspect a lot of those men are wanted or should be. So watch your back. And be careful."

"I'll be the best blamed lawman you ever had. Just get my name back for me."

"There's one thing you got to understand. Those badges are going to make you targets."

Bronco chuckled. "Marshal, me and Curly been nothin' but targets for fifteen years."

Bronco downed his coffee and went to bed. For a while, Cord's face danced before his eyes. But he was exhausted and sore and weary, and he had a badge. He slept deep for the first time in many a year.

When Curly came in, the lawman was asleep on the bunk near the stove in the kitchen, but he didn't care. Curly was singing and dancing and hollering. Norton grunted and turned over on the bunk, his back to Curly.

Curly spun into the other room and sat on Bronco.

"Wake up, dang it."

"What the devil's the matter with you?"

"I just had the best time of my life, that's what."

"Well, simmer down and get some sleep. We got a big job ahead of us tomorrow."

Curly laughed and got up, dancing over to his bunk and plunking down fully clothed. Within minutes, he was snoring.

At daylight, Randy was fixing breakfast, with Norton helping. Bronco was so sore and stiff he could hardly walk, and he put his hand on Curly's shoulder to get into the kitchen.

"Wow," Randy said, "the marshal told me how you both was gonna be deputies. That's gonna make the town happy, but the Sladeks are gonna hate it."

"You know who owns that old building by the bridge?" Norton asked the youth.

"Nobody. It was an express office, but it closed down when the company pulled out. Later on, the other one opened up."

"Then nobody will care if we have a look," Norton said.

"Nope."

Bronco leaned back in his chair, shoving his hat back as he spoke thoughtfully. "We got another problem you can help us with, Marshal."

And Bronco, with Curly's help, gave the hypothetical story of a schoolteacher who kept the money meant for a fancy school and taught the child herself.

"Well," Norton said, "you'd need a little more

information than that. But if she was some kind of certified schoolteacher, she'd have a good argument. If there was nothin' in writing, she'd have a little more on her side."

"Would you arrest her first?" Bronco asked.

"No, I wouldn't. I figure the burden's on the one who sent her the money. He'd have to have documented evidence of his intent and would have to prove that this schoolteacher clearly understood. If he made out bank drafts to her and not the school, I don't think he has much of a case."

Curly smiled. "Sounds good to me."

While the men talked for hours Charity was up at the rooming house with Freddie in her room, and Elva was in another room with Emmy Lou. The three Sladek men had bunked downstairs near the hearth, and the round, rosy Mrs. Bromley was telling them to get out of the way so she could clean up their mess.

Frank glared at her as he sat up from his blankets. "I hope you cook better than you talk."

"I hope you smell better than you look," she retorted.

Frank grunted and watched her head for the kitchen, then he smiled. "Fine-lookin' woman."

Leo and Lucas sat up, rubbing their eyes.

"Man alive," Lucas said. "Have I got a big head."

"And nothin' in it," Frank said.

But when they sat down at Mrs. Bromley's breakfast feast, the men were amazed. Frank had three helpings of biscuits to go with his second helping of bacon and eggs.

The woman frowned. "Well, now I have to make more biscuits for the ladies."

"Forget about them," Frank said. "You got any more?"

"Maybe a couple."

"Well, bring 'em out, woman."

"Woman, huh. Just don't forget to pay me."

He grinned as she went back to the kitchen, but Leo and Lucas were still grumpy. The two got up and went, outside into the cold morning air.

"Neither one of us is gonna get Charity," Leo said. "Not unless we get rid of Bronco. She's still makin' cow eyes at him. His winnin' that shootin' contest and ridin' ole Trigger Foot didn't help much."

"And Cord didn't do his job."

"Yeah, that was a real surprise."

They fell silent as their father came out, patting his middle. "Boys, that woman can really cook. Too bad I'm already married."

"Pa, we got to do somethin' about Bronco."

"Forget it, boys. Anything you do, she'll hate."

"But she'll get over it," Lucas said.

"Some things folks never get over. Like havin' my best friend hanged behind my back. A man who saved my life at Savannah."

"What are you talkin' about, Pa?" asked Lucas.

"A man who trusted me."

"Who, Pa?"

"Rad Hodges, who else?"

"But you can't hold that against us. Hooper started the whole thing," Leo said warily."And that was over fifteen, sixteen years ago. Why bring it up now?"

"I don't know. Somethin', somehow, I ain't sure, but it's been on my mind since yesterday."

Frank shrugged his big shoulders. "Well, let's go on down to look at the horses and see if old Trigger Foot got out. I don't feel like listenin' to your stepmother's chatter."

As the three Sladeks headed for the livery, Norton and his new deputies were jerking off the boards at the old express office. Randy was helping and had brought a can of white paint.

Inside, they saw the vault in the back with a row of steel bars and a door protecting its access.

"Just like a cell," Bronco said.

"Sure enough is," Norton agreed. "And you got a desk besides. And a stove. And you even got a couple of bunks."

"Front windows got bars," Bronco added.

"It ain't much," Norton said, "and neither is your forty a month, but you're gonna be mighty proud of what you're doing."

While Randy painted the sign "U.S. Marshal" on a board, the three men set about cleaning up the office and sweeping it out. They found the keys to the steel door and the vault, which was empty.

When the Sladeks came back from the livery, they heard hammering down the street. "What the devil?" Frank said with a grunt.

They walked down the boardwalk and paused in dismay when they saw Randy put the last nail in the sign above the door. The youth turned and grinned, then went back inside.

"I saw a stranger," Leo said. "That's probably him."

"Well, boys, we'd best go make him welcome."

"He's gonna cramp our style," Lucas said.

"What you forget, boys, is that these marshals have hundreds of miles to cover. We ain't gonna see him more' n once a year."

They paused just outside as Norton came out, his hat pushed back from his wide brow. "Gentlemen?"

"We're the Sladeks," Frank said. "We're glad you're here."

"Marshal Norton, but I'm ridin' out by noon."

"Sorry to hear that."

"I'm leavin' two deputies."

Frank and his sons stared as Curly and Bronco came outside, badges on their vests in the morning sunlight, both grinning lazily.

Lucas and Leo stood with their mouths open.

Frank recovered. "Well, good."

The lawmen went back inside, and Randy paused to grin before following them in and closing the door behind them.

Frank rubbed his chin. "Well, that's a kicker."

His sons let him walk up to the rooming house alone, and they wandered off down the street where people were beginning to stir.

"One saloon and no church," Lucas growled. "But we got two lawmen."

"Not for long."

"Ain't you afraid of Norton?"

"Not if he can't prove nothin'," said Frank.

"So what are we gonna do?" Lucas asked.

"Like I said, Hooper and his men will do anything for money."

THIRTEEN

Three weeks after Norton had ridden out, nothing had changed. Freddie made frequent trips to the ranch to keep Charity safe, but Charity was kept at the ranch at all times. No letter had come to Frank Sladek from his late sister.

There was no obvious crime, no one to arrest. Young Randy came often to play cards, and Sally came just as often to drag him back off to some doings. The only real news was that a preacher had set up shop in a house in back of the saloon.

Bronco and Curly sat in their office one afternoon, browsing through the two law books and the stack of Wanted posters that Norton had left, along with a dispatch pouch that had come through on the stage.

Bronco was behind the desk and put his boots up high on it, leaning back in the wooden swivel chair as he opened the leather pouch and took out all the papers.

"This is the life," Bronco said.

"Yeah, well, lawmen get shot all the time."

"We was gonna get shot anyway. Now we're gettin' paid for it."

Curly went to the stove where the coffee was brewing. "Freddie likes my badge. Too bad Charity never got to see yours. They don't even let her come to town."

"I'm glad Freddie's lookin' in on her."

"Freddie says Frank is good to Charity. And she says he's her legal guardian."

"But she's twenty-five years old."

"Yeah, but Charity has a lot of loyalty to ole Frank. She did tell Freddie that Leo and Lucas are mighty restless. Frank's holdin' back their shares and makin' 'em miserable. Charity told her there was plenty goin' on between them and Hooper."

"What kind of goin's on?"

"Charity wasn't sure."

"It's a peaceable town, Curly. The only problems we're gonna have is with the Sladeks. Reckon Frank never got that letter from his sister."

"Well, like Freddy says, bank drafts were made to her and there was nothin' in writing. She was a certified teacher and saw no wrong in what she was doing. Even if that letter shows up, ain't nothin' Frank can prove."

"Hey, there's a sealed letter in here from Norton."

"Yeah?" Curly came over to the desk and pulled up a chair. "What's it say?"

"Let's see. Good grief. Listen…

Dear Marshals Hodges and Haines:

I received a telegram back from Texas. No official charges were ever made against Jim Hodges for murder or Wiley Haines for rustling. No reports were ever made to the Rangers, probably because the Rangers were already looking for evidence against the Sladeks, who were suspected of numerous crimes.

This means you can use your real names if you so choose. They have no information on who killed your father or the other small ranchers. They believe they were hanged to make it look like they had been caught rustling, so no one would question it.

Meanwhile, I have included more

Wanted posters in this dispatch. Please pay particular attention to the one on Esther Stanley.
Good luck, men.
Marshal Philip Norton

Curly whistled softly. "Bronco, do you know what this means?"

"It means we're free men, Curly. You got that? Free."

"That deserves another cup of coffee."

Curly danced over to the stove and refilled their cups while Bronco reread the letter over and over. Curly whistled again and again. He sat down, and he had Bronco read the letter out loud one more time.

Then Curly sipped his coffee and leaned back.

"Holy cow, Bronco. I mean Jim. Jim Hodges. Jimmy. Little Jimmy."

"Freddie's gonna like that," Bronco said, grinning.

"Bronco Jim Hodges. And Curly Wiley Haines."

"Now Frank Sladek will know who we are."

Curly nodded. "But he can't do nothin', except try to hide who killed your pa. And maybe take some kind of outlaw revenge for you killing his sons."

Bronco sobered. "Yeah."

"Maybe you won't want to use your real name."

"I'm Bronco Jim Hodges, and that's it."

"Okay, but right now, I'm gonna run up and tell Freddie."

"Yeah, go ahead."

For a short time, Bronco Jim Hodges sat staring at the letter, tears stinging his eyes. Free men. After fifteen years. But he still didn't know who had killed his father. The trouble was, Sladek would know he was the man who had killed his sons. Now there was going to be an explosion in the valley, but Bronco didn't care.

Up at the boardinghouse on the front porch, Curly was sitting in a chair, fussing and complaining as Freddie first used scissors and then a razor, but little by little, the beard came off.

"My, oh, my," Freddie said, sponging off his face with a wet towel. "Just look at you, Curly Wiley Haines."

"I look okay, huh?"

She held a little mirror for him to see. "Remember, I told you I'd marry you if you'd shave."

Curly stared into the mirror, suddenly awkward. "Well, uh, you was just kiddin'."

She bent over and kissed him full on the lips. Curly's feet went straight up in the air and he gripped the chair arms. She slowly drew back, and his face was crimson.

"Am I just kidding?" she asked.

"Holy smoke."

"So what do you think?"

"Well, I got money saved up, me and Bronco, and I got a job, and I got my name back. But the Sladeks might still gun me down."

"I have a black dress."

He stared up at her. "You mean, you want to marry an old fool like me, knowin' everything?"

"You're a young man, Curly."

When Curly came back to the office, he was whistling. Bronco sat up straight, staring at the strong chin, wide mouth and skinny nose. His upper cheeks were tan from the sun, but he was white and had red razor scrapes from there down to his chin.

"What a sight," Bronco said in dismay.

"Freddie done it." Curly danced around and poured himself another cup of coffee. "She kissed me right on the lips. And we're gettin' married right soon."

Bronco stared at his friend. "I never thought you would make the jump."

"It was a heck of a lot easier than I thought."

As Curly sat down, Bronco grinned and shuffled the papers. "We'll put that letter in the vault back there, since we got the key."

"Good idea. I'll do it right now, after you read it aloud four or five times more."

"You know, Curly, you oughta learn to read."

"Well, I can read a little bit. But Freddie's gonna teach me after we're hitched." Curly took the letter to the vault and locked it up, then returned for more coffee.

Bronco grinned, then leaned forward as he picked up one of the handbills."Here it is. Esther Stanley."

"Yeah? What's it say?"

"Well, it seems this here Esther Stanley was a widow who married a Walter Stanley in Philadelphia and left him for dead. He filed charges but she had already taken his money and disappeared. She's changed her name and been widowed a few more times since Stanley put detectives on her. Seems like they figure her husbands were poisoned just like Stanley was. Anyway, Stanley's her legal husband."

"Nice lady."

"Let's see. She travels with a daughter. And she recently married…"

"Yeah, come on. Let's have it," Curly said, excited.

"…Frank Sladek in Texas."

"Holy smoke."

"Elva Sladek is Esther Stanley, a widow maker."

Curly grinned. "Should we be in a hurry to arrest her?"

"We can't put it off. Takes a day to get there. We'll saddle up before dawn and go take care of this little detail."

Curly could scarcely contain himself. "Frank Sladek married to a widow maker."

The door swung open, and a lanky man in sloppy clothes and a battered hat was standing there, swaying, trying to catch his breath.

The lawmen stood up, and the man staggered over to take Curly's chair, sprawling himself and breathing hard.

"Who the devil are you?" Curly asked.

"Hawkins. Got me a farm west of here, right up against Sladek's place. Four of 'em ran some cattle right over my grass and over to my waterholes, muddyin' 'em up and knockin' down some fence I had around some com and ruinin' half of that."

"Well," Bronco said thoughtfully. "I guess that's trespass, all right."

"It's murder."

"What?"

"One of my sons tried to stop them, and some skinny fellow and another man shot him clean through. They didn't see me comin' through the trees about then. Nothin' I could do for my boy and there was four of 'em, so I hid until they took off with the cattle. But next thing I knowed, when I was headed back to the house, I stopped and looked around, and they stopped on the ridge and saw me. I was scared they was comin' back, but they didn't."

"So they know there was a witness," Curly said.

"You'd recognize these men?" Bronco asked.

"Yeah, when I was hidin' in the trees, they was talkin'. The ones that done it was called Boney and Hooper. The other two, I don't know. Their names wasn't used."

"Boney and Hooper," Curly echoed as he poured the man a cup of coffee.

"When did this happen?" Bronco asked.

"This mornin'. What are you gonna do about it?"

Bronco was thoughtful. "Have you fill out an affidavit so we can arrest them. We got no judge to sign any warrants."

"Take us a day to get out to Sladek's house," Curly said. "How far is it to your place, Mr. Hawkins?"

"About three hours. Ain't you afraid they'll get away?"

Bronco shook his head. "Those fellas just figure the law applies to everybody but them. First we'll swing by your place and make sure your family's all right."

Bronco took up the Wanted poster on Esther Stanley and put it in his inside vest pocket. After making up bedrolls and saddling up, and after Curly told Freddie, they rode out with Hawkins to see where the cattle had muddied his water and killed his son. Bronco leaned on the horn and pushed his hat back.

"They're tryin' to tell you somethin', Mr. Hawkins."

"Sladek tried to buy me out. Now he's tryin' to scare me off. Well, I got one more son, and we ain't goin' nowhere."

Curly and Bronco spent the night at Hawkins's place, determined to see justice done the next day.

Charity paced in her room at the big house on Sladek's ranch. When she went down for supper, she learned that the new housekeeper, a big swarthy woman, had prepared a splendid meal in the dining room, where a crystal chandelier, newly arrived, was dangling from the ceiling.

Elva was playing the queen and Emmy Lou the princess.

The two Sladek boys sat on either side of Charity, each fighting for her attention. Frank sat at the head of the table, and later; when they were enjoying their coffee in front of the hearth, he had plenty to say.

"I got to hand it to that Bronco, winnin' that match and ridin' old Trigger Foot. Now what are we gonna do with that old roan?"

"Nobody else can ride Trigger Foot," Leo said. "And we won't let Bronco on 'im again. We'll still make plenty of money off that roan, you can bet on it."

Lucas frowned. "He was lucky, that's all."

"He's a legend," Charity said.

"He's gonna be a dead legend one of these days," Leo said.

"He's wearing a badge," she reminded him.

"So what?"

"My, my," Elva said. "Such talk."

And she proceeded to tell stories of Philadelphia and all the other fine places and how they were going to lord it over everyone in the valley. Emmy Lou primped and fussed with her hair and flirted with Lucas.

Charity suddenly stood up and went out on the porch, closing the door behind her, sick of the conversation. Leo followed her, closing the door behind him. She gazed up at the stars, her heart pounding with the cry of a distant, lone coyote.

"Go away, Leo."

He came close to her. "It's gonna be me and you, Charity. All you have to do is set the date."

"I'm not ready for marriage."

"You got that Bronco on your mind."

"No, I haven't."

"I'll kill 'im."

She turned slowly, her face burning. "No, please, Leo. There's nothing to it. I promise you."

"You ain't fallin' for him?"

"Of course not. Uncle Frank's made it clear I have to marry you or Lucas."

"Well, it's gonna be me."

He grabbed her, and she struggled, but he pulled her against him and gave her a wet, sloppy kiss. Breathless, she drew back, but he wouldn't release her, his hands tight on her arms.

"And you'd better agree," he growled, "or Bronco's a dead man."

"You leave him alone."

"Yeah? Just because he's wearin' that fancy badge?"

She squirmed free and headed for the front door. He grabbed her from behind and spun her back into his arms, mauling her.

"Let me go!"

He began kissing her hungrily, and she fought him. Abruptly the door opened, and Frank Sladek stood there framed in the light that fell on the struggling couple and Charity's frantic attempt to escape.

"Back off, Leo."

Leo laughed and let her go. "I was just funnin', Pa."

"You ever see me treat your ma like that? Get inside, Charity."

She ran past Frank and collided with a surprised Lucas, backing off and moving around him, then hurrying up the stairs, only to run into Elva, who was snickering. "So that's the kind of a woman you are," the older woman said.

Charity gave her a dirty look and rushed to her room.

She latched the door and fell onto her bed in the pale light of the moon through her window, tears running down her face as she tried to calm down. Then she heard a loud noise.

Going to the window, she looked down toward the porch and saw Frank and Leo fighting, pounding each other with fists. She turned down the lamp, then slowly lifted the windowpane, staring down at the furious struggle.

Then Leo went flying and landed on his rear, sliding in the dirt. He didn't get up but lay there panting. She heard the door slam as Frank went inside and Lucas came out.

Lucas went to stand over his brother.

"Pa sure whupped you."

"He'll never get a chance to do it again."

"Cool down, Leo."

"He's gonna pay for this."

"What are you gonna do?"

"I'm gonna look in that tin box tonight, that's what."

"Hold on, here come Hooper and Boney, and they look mighty annoyed about somethin'."

Charity drew a deep breath and slowly closed

the window. The large tin box with the will had been dangled in front of everyone. She sat down on the bed, her face in her hands.

In the late morning of the following day, Bronco and Curly came riding up the trail to the ranch, Winchesters across their pommels, eyes watching the hills and pines.

As they neared the house and corrals and numerous, outbuildings, they reined up.

"Fancy place," Curly said. "But I don't see nobody. No horses. Nothin'. Just that old mule. And that team hitched to the wagon up by the house."

As they neared the front porch, Elva came running out of the house, frantic and waving her hands. Emmy Lou came out with her, hugging herself. The housekeeper followed, her hands over her mouth.

Tom Tyree and Billy came out behind them, both with rifles. "Lord a'mighty," Billy said. "We're glad to see you."

"What happened?" Bronco asked.

"Me and Tom and Krinkle, we come ridin' in from the line shack this mornin'. Found Mr. Sladek shot. Leo and Lucas took off with Hooper and Boney and two other men, Topper and Target. They took sixty head of horses, includin' them fancy brood mares. After they tied up the women here. Reckon they figure they can travel fast if they just took them horses, which are worth a heap of money."

Curly frowned. "Where are the rest of the men?"

"A long way north with the herd. In the meadows.

Even Biscuit's up there with the chuck wagon."

"Who shot Frank Sladek?" Bronco asked.

"Leo done it."

"They were all having an argument," Elva said. "We could hear Leo shouting something about money. We were all coming down the stairs when Frank pulled a gun, and Leo shot him. Lucas was there. And Hooper and Boney."

"Where's Charity?"

Emmy Lou put her fingers to her lips. "They took her."

"What?"

"Leo grabbed her when we came down. He hit her with his fist, and she curled right up. He threw her over his shoulder and went out the door. Hooper and Boney tied us up. And the housekeeper too. They all thought Frank was dead. So did we."

"They must know they can't get away with it," Curly growled.

"The tin box with the will," Elva said. "It was open and on the floor. We're too frightened to stay here, so we'll be going to Mrs. Bromley's until we see if Frank lives through this. But I want you to arrest Leo and Lucas as soon as you can and lock them up."

Bronco frowned at her and swung down from the saddle. He tossed the reins over the hitching rail and went inside the house, Curly following.

Frank Sladek had been placed on the couch and was bleeding through bandages on his chest, but he was alive.

"Bronco," he said, his face pale but anger flashing in his eyes. "They got Charity."

"What was the fight about?"

"Close the door."

Curly went back and closed it while Bronco went down on one knee next to him, and Curly stood back, quiet. They were alone with Frank, who was breathing heavily and with difficulty.

"Well?"

"They found the will, along with some bank ledgers and some ten thousand in greenbacks. The will left one-third to Charity and gave them a third each. But I had put a lot of money in her name down in some Texas banks. I knew she'd be marryin' one of my sons anyhow, so it'd still be in the family. But when he saw the ledgers, and their names wasn't on it—"

"That made Leo mad?" Bronco asked.

"He exploded and started to attack me, so I pulled my gun to hold 'im off. Leo drew real fast and shot me. I reckon they left thinkin' I was dead. And all because I put Charity's name in those books. Maybe I was just a sentimental old fool, but she gave me more pleasure than my sons ever did."

Bronco leaned closer. "But she wasn't your daughter."

"No, but I'd been widowed a long time when I fell for her mother. Her name was Charity too, but she turned me down. She married Wiley Haines and had a little girl. After she died, her pa threw the child away. I took her in and called her Charity."

"Threw her away?!" Curly growled, eyes blazing.

Bronco started to rise. "Curly—"

But Curly thrust him aside and knelt in a fury, grabbing Frank's arm and shaking it. "Look at me, Sladek. You stole my ranch. My wife died because we was livin' off the land.

I couldn't take care of my little girl, so I left her at the church. But you got her, you dirty rotten thief. And then your boys tried to hang me for brandin' an old skinny maverick."

Frank was dazed from loss of blood, but he stared at Corly's shaven face in dismay. "Haines? Wiley Haines?"

"That's right."

"You went off with Jim Hodges and his gang."

"Jim Hodges was a fifteen-year-old boy. He come ridin' on the hangin' all by hisself, and when he tried' to stop it, your three sons pulled down on him and tried to blow him away. He got all three of them. But there was no gang. Not ever."

"Hooper said—"

"You're a fool, Sladek."

"But I didn't know—"

"Yeah, well, it was self-defense, but that boy would've had plenty of reasons to kill Sladeks if he had known you'd hung his pa."

"No, I didn't. Rad Hodges saved my life in the war. I never would have done it. I was plenty mad when I found out."

"So who did it?"

"It was Leo and Hooper and some of the boys."

"And what'd you do about it?" Curly demanded.

"Leo was my son. And I was tryin' to own half of Texas."

"And you didn't care how you got it."

Frank closed his eyes. "You're right. I let it all happen. You got to get her back, Haines."

"She's my daughter, Frank."

"I know."

"And this is Bronco Jim Hodges."

Frank looked up to stare at Bronco, who knelt beside Curly. "You?"

"I come back to find out who hanged my pa. Now I know."

"Jimmy Hodges? That skinny little kid? That's you?"

"I've been hidin' out for fifteen years. But I ain't hidin' no more. Marshal Norton got our names cleared."

Frank had tears in his eyes. "You're Rad's boy. Rad carried me a mile on his back at Savannah with my blood runnin' all over him. Your father was the best friend I ever had. I loved him like a brother."

"He told me about savin' you."

"Forgive me, Jimmy. I was wrong to let my boys loose."

Bronco swallowed. "Pa would forgive you right off, so I reckon I got no choice. But Leo's goin' to jail."

"I guess I never treated them boys right. I pulled a gun on him. He shot in self-defense."

"It wasn't self-defense when he hanged my father."

Frank closed his eyes, wincing in worsening pain.

He pressed his hands to his chest, and more blood oozed through the bandages.

"We got somethin' else to tell you," Bronco said."Seems your wife is still married to some Walter Stanley back east. She poisoned 'im and left 'im for dead, taking his money. Then she went on and took care of a few more husbands. They followed her trail to Texas. You were next, Frank."

Curly nodded. "She was going to poison you the minute she figured out how to get your money. When we get back, we're gonna arrest her and her daughter. If we don't make it, you get ahold of Norton. But in the meantime, I sure wouldn't let her feed you anything."

"Or give you anything to drink," Bronco added.

Frank didn't look up for a moment. He lay

still, his hands on his wounds, and then a slow smile crossed his lips. He looked up with a new glow on his face, and now, despite his pain, he was grinning.

"That's the best news I've had all day."

Krinkle opened the door and came inside. "Tom says Mrs. Bromley does some doctoring. We'll take him on in."

"We could use another gun," Bronco said, rising. Krinkle made a face. "The Tyree brothers—"

"Are too young to die," Bronco said to Finish Krinkle's sentence.

Krinkle nodded. "You're right. Who's gonna miss an old-timer like me?"

"We got to get that mule loaded out there," Curly said.

"And more ammunition," Bronco added.

Krinkle wiped his mouth. "Well, there's six of them and three of us. That's about even."

Curly and Krinkle went on out the door, but Bronco paused to pull a blanket up over Frank, who turned his head to look up at him.

"Be careful, Jimmy. They've all crossed the line, and they ain't givin' up easy."

FOURTEEN

With the Tyree boys taking the wounded Frank and the frantic women to town in the wagon, Bronco, Curly, and Krinkle outfitted themselves, packing the mule with food and water and extra ammunition.

"They'll be moving fast," Krinkle said. "That's why they didn't take any cattle. They can run them' horses right along with 'em. They'll follow the river south and avoid the army post."

And Leo was leading the way fast, hardly giving the horses time to graze along the river. The men were in a hurry, wearing out their horses as they went. The grassy land was dotted with trees, and cottonwoods and brush lined the river. It was low, rolling land, and the horses had nothing to slow them down.

"It was a fair fight," Leo said one night by

the fire.

Lucas nodded. "Stop hatin' yourself. Pa pulled a gun on you, and you thought he was gonna kill you."

"There he was, dead on the floor. My own pa. And that Elva woman screamin' we was gonna hang for it. I sure wasn't stickin' around to be arrested."

Lucas leaned back on his saddle, staring up at the black sky. "What does it matter, Leo? Before we was twenty, we'd already hanged a man and shot a half dozen men. We was born to hang."

"Yeah, but it was all to get land, remember? Land and money for us, Pa always said. Well, it wasn't for us. All the money was for Charity."

"But all we got to do is marry her, and we get her share of the ranch and all the money. Besides, it ain't easy for a woman to claim an inheritance. Especially when she ain't even kin."

They paused to look at the weary Charity, who was asleep by the cottonwood nearest the river. She looked so lovely in the starlight, they stared a moment longer.

"We got to stay with the will," Leo said. "We don't want that Elva woman claimin' anything.

Now I figure I'm the one to marry Charity."

"She ain't never gonna forgive you for shootin' Frank. So it's got to be me."

"We'll let her choose when we find a preacher."

"Meanwhile, Bronco and Curly are bound to come after us," Lucas said.

"Two men? We'll pick 'em off like flies. They ain't gettin' no help out of that chicken town. And we got four men with us, all of 'em loyal."

"Hooper and Boney come along because they figure on gettin' hanged for that killin' at that Hawkins's place. They'd figured on gettin' some of the cattle, but they was too scared not to run off with us. And Topper and Target come because they were along when Hawkins's boy got it."

"Reckon old Krinkle's gonna be mad, missin' out." Leo folded his arms, kicking dirt at the fire. "You know, Lucas, what it said in that will, that she was Wiley Haines's daughter. How come he never told us?"

"Didn't want her to find out, I reckon. Didn't want her chasin' after some outlaw his own sons nearly hanged."

"I seen Haines's wife once. She was right pretty. But she died of lung fever. When Pa heard about it, he started tearing the house apart. We thought he was crazy, remember?"

"Yeah, I reckon that's why he give the money to Charity, but it still wasn't right. He was an old fool," Lucas said.

As they talked Charity listened with her eyes closed, stunned by their words. Her father had been an outlaw? That would explain why she had been abandoned, left behind for a better life. Tears came to her eyes, and she lay wondering how she was going to get away, because that was exactly what she was planning to do.

It was two days before the lawmen caught up with the herd and watched from a distance in a grove of aspens on a hill. They could see six men herding the horses, following the river south, a wandering stream lined with brush and cottonwoods. Charity was riding between two of them.

Krinkle spat and tugged at his hat brim. "Well, now, how are we gonna get 'em?"

"It ain't gonna be easy," Bronco said.

"A stampede would keep 'em busy," Curly said.

Krinkle frowned. "I hate doin' that to mares in foal."

"You got a better idea?"

"Yeah. I could ride in like I was mad bein' left out, and I could get the word to her."

"Not a bad idea," Bronco said. "They'll be camping along the river, all right. You ride in there tonight, get settled. Curly can get on the other side of the river and head farther down, then cross over and hide in the cottonwoods some place ahead of their next camp. Come suppertime tomorrow, I'll ride in real bold. Curly can get behind 'em. Before the shootin' starts, you get Charity across the river."

That evening, Krinkle went riding into the camp. Leo and Lucas were having supper and stood up to look him over. Charity was in her blankets, sitting by a big cottonwood near the water, watching.

"Where'd you come from?" Leo asked.

"I've been tryin' to catch up." Krinkle swung down from the saddle. "Ain't like you to leave me out of this. I come all the way from Texas with you boys. I want my share."

"All right. Have some supper."

"Thanks."

"Anybody on our trail?"

"Didn't wait around."

"Didn't see no marshals?"

"Nope, just Elva and her daughter runnin' around in circles. The Tyree boys was takin' Frank's body to town."

As Krinkle sat down to eat, Leo and Lucas mounted up to take a turn at night herding, and Leo leaned from the saddle.

"You relieve Hooper in a couple hours, so get some sleep."

The brothers rode out toward the milling herd, and Krinkle spoke without turning. "Don't look around, Miss Charity."

She stiffened and didn't move.

"Bronco and Curly are comin' tomorrow night. When the fightin' starts, you has got to get across the river."

"I can't swim."

"Then grab my horse. I'll leave it saddled near you."

Charity was shivering with excitement and dread. She didn't want Curly or Bronco to die, but she didn't want to stay here either.

The following evening, they again camped along the river. Everyone was night herding except Krinkle, Lucas, and Target, a wiry man with beady eyes. The wind was rising, and the men were worried about keeping the horses contained.

Krinkle was saddling his horse to take a turn. Charity was twenty feet away by a cottonwood, right on the river bank. Target was in his blankets, about to bed down. Lucas was finishing his supper when he tensed.

"Somebody's comin'."

"Just one of the boys," Krinkle said.

Lucas stared as Bronco rode right up to the campfire and reined up with no firearms showing, just his badge gleaming in the moonlight. They couldn't hear the pounding of his heart or see the sweat on his back.

"Well, Marshal," Lucas said, a little too loud. "You come to arrest us for drivin' our own horses?"

"Leo shot your father, and you're an accessory."

"That was a fair fight. He pulled a gun on Leo."

"And you both took a woman against her will. That's false imprisonment. Hooper and Boney killed one of your neighbors. By takin' them along with you, you're aidin' and abettin'. I'm takin' you all back."

"You and what army?"

"I don't need an army to arrest a couple of Sladeks. My real name is Jim Hodges."

Lucas dropped his plate and let his hands fall to his sides. His eyes were round. "Hodges? You killed three of my brothers."

"They tried to kill me."

"The law only works against Sladeks, is that right?"

Bronco remained in the saddle, his gaze fixed on Lucas, but aware that in the background, Krinkle was leading his horse and Charity to the river.

"You forget," Bronco said, "that Leo and Hooper also murdered Rad Hodges, my father."

Anger was rising in Lucas. "I didn't have nothin' to do with that. But right now, I'm gonna make you sorry you killed my brothers."

"It was self-defense," Bronco said. "Like now."

There was a long moment when Lucas stood with his hands at his side. Target was sitting up in his blankets, and the way his face was twisted, Bronco knew he had his revolver out of the holster.

Lucas suddenly pulled his six-gun, tiring, even as Bronco whipped out his own Colt and fired back, so close together it sounded like one shot. Lucas gasped, a bullet in his chest.

He dropped to his knees, eyes glazed, then fell flat on his face, arms sprawled in death.

Target showed his gun, but before he could pull the trigger, Krinkle spun and shot him through the head.

Three men were coming full gallop out of the night. Hooper and Boney were in the lead. With them was a thin, scrawny man. All were armed and firing fast and furious.

Bullets whistled by Bronco's ear.

Bronco swung from the saddle and slapped his buckskin on the rump, sending it off. He and Krinkle dived for the trees and took cover, firing back as the men charged.

Krinkle got Boney, who flew off the saddle and landed on the campfire, groaned, and rolled off, only to die as he clasped his chest with blood all over his hands.

Bronco shot Hooper as the outlaw roared with fury. The big man lifted half out of the saddle, then spun his horse around.

Curly, appearing on horseback, shot the third man.

Hooper's horse shied and jumped aside when it was turned into the campfire and on top of Boney. The wounded Hooper leaned crazily from the saddle, trying to hold on, and then he fell, rolling twice before ending up on his back, his six-gun still in his hand.

Bronco ran over and stood over him.

"Hooper, you ain't gonna die just yet. I want you to know I'm Jim Hodges. You and Leo murdered my father."

The man knew he was dying, but he glared up at Bronco.

"Hodges? Yeah, your old man, huh?"

"That's right."

"Good."

Then Hooper died, his mouth still open as if he had planned to add some threats. Bronco drew a deep breath, his stomach churning. Sixteen years ago men had brutally murdered his father. This ugly man had been one of them.

Yet Bronco was nauseated.

Curly came to his side. "Where's Charity?"

Krinkle joined them. "She's waitin' across the river."

It was then that Bronco drew himself up and looked around. "But where's Leo?"

FIFTEEN

Bronco stared at Hooper's body and put his boot on the man's shoulder, rolling him over so he did not have to look at that face in the firelight.

Then he and Curly rode out looking for Leo while Krinkle stayed behind to watch for him and also dragged the bodies away from the camp.

Most of the horses had their rumps to the rising wind, heads down. It was a cold night with stars and a full moon.

"He's plumb gone," Curly said.

"We'll get 'im. Tomorrow."

They rode back to camp, where Krinkle was waiting. "I'll get Charity," Bronco said.

Curly shook his head. "I'll get her."

"I ain't surprised Leo took off," Krinkle said.

Curly rode on across the river while Bronco

was discovering how tired he was.

"I'll take care of the herd," Krinkle said. "Soon's I get my horse back."

Curly yelled from across the river, his voice echoing in the night. "She's gone!"

Bronco swung into the saddle and set his buckskin into the icy water, charging across in a fury. He reined up at the bank, then carefully rode up to save the signs.

"Here's where she was kneelin'," Curly said.

Bronco dismounted and let the moonlight fill in the shape of the land. "She was knocked down and dragged to her horse."

"Leo must have her," Curly growled.

Bronco walked farther along the river, all the way south to the bend, following the prints that led to the bank.

"They crossed back over," Bronco said. "He's headed for those mountains. But if we go afore sunup, we'll lose the trail."

"Krinkle can stay with the herd."

Furious, the two lawmen headed east at first light with the pack mule. The trail was getting harder to follow in the rocks and trees as the country grew more rugged.

"He could set himself up and pick us off," Curly said.

They were forced to camp that night to avoid losing the trail. They made no fire, but sat in the dark, listening to the night sounds.

"Frank knows who we both are," Curly said. "What do you think he'll do?"

"If he's still alive, nothing."

"Do you think he'll tell her?"

"Yeah, I do."

"All that time, we was tryin' to get away from the trail herd, but things kept happenin' to hold us. Then we finally get clear and run into Freddie, and we go back in the quicksand again. Next thing we knowed, Norton comes along and fixes us up with these badges."

"And now we're free men."

Bronco took first watch, and as Curly slept he stared into the night, thinking about Charity and how she was being dragged along by Leo. It made him furious, but all he could do was grit his teeth.

Charity was sitting by a tree, staring into the darkness. Her hands were tied behind her, the rope reaching to Leo's wrist. Blankets were wrapped around her, but she was cold. Her wrists were burning from the hair rope. Leo lay nearby, snoring quietly.

At dawn, Leo sat up and yawned. "You all right, Charity?"

"You have to let me go, Leo."

"Not a chance. I got a fistful of money, but we still have to get what's in those Texas banks."

"You can have it. I'll sign it over to you. Just let me go."

"We're gonna get hitched, and that's it. Now be quiet or I'll figure a way to shut you up."

She looked away quickly. He had not had time to bother her much on the trail, but she dreaded reaching some hiding place. Her jaw and cheek hurt from his blows, and she ached from the saddle, but she'd rather keep going than have him turn his attention to her.

Bronco and Curly were already on the trail. Bending from the saddle as he rode in the lead, Bronco could see the bent blades of grass and stones rolled out of their sockets, and the cracked tree branches and scratches on rocks they had passed.

Scratches probably made by Charity's outthrust boot.

"They're going up to that ridge," Bronco said, reining up. "He'll have a bead on us from there."

"Then we got to get there first."

"I'll go. You follow with the pack mule, real slow. Make sure I'm up there afore you get within range."

"Be careful."

Bronco turned his horse off the trail and took off through the trees at a trot, praying the sound would not carry. He urged his horse up the steep grade, sometimes walking and leading, desperate to reach the ridge before Leo did.

He was successful and left his horse in the trees and brush, then moved on foot to take cover in the rocks on the south side of the trail. Now he saw them riding up the grade.

Charity was in the lead, and Leo was right behind her with his rifle across the pommel, constantly looking back down the trail.

As Charity made the ridge, Leo called out.

"Rein up over there and take cover behind me."

She obeyed, and he dismounted, swatting the horses to send them back into the trees. Then he knelt with his rifle at the edge of the boulders on the north side of the trail, opposite where Bronco was hiding and a few feet in front of where Charity was kneeling.

"What are you doing?" she asked.

"I'm gonna blow a hole in the first man shows up."

Frantic, she jumped up and before he could react, she grabbed the rifle barrel, trying to pull it free, but he sprang to his feet and slammed his fist in her face. She staggered backward and fell on her side, rolling. She struggled to rise but was too shaken, so she crawled to his side.

"Leave them alone, Leo."

"Who, that bearded old Curly and that fancy Bronco?"

"They're wearing badges."

"So what? Now get down flat so they won't see you."He put his hand on her head and forced her down at his side.

Furious, Bronco sprang to his feet. "Drop it, Leo."

Startled, Leo spun around and grabbed Charity by the hair, then jerked her up in front of him and pulled his six-gun in his right hand, locking her wrists in front of her with his left.

"Drop it, Bronco, or I'll blow a hole in her."

"You'd die just as fast, Leo."

"Big talk, Bronco."

"I'm arrestin' you for the murder of my father. Look at me, Leo. Take a good look."

"I ain't never seen you before."

"I'm Jim Hodges."

Leo moistened his lips, his face darkening.

"Well, now. I reckon I got to finish the job."

Charity squirmed in Leo's grasp. His left hand was clamped on her small wrists, held against her waist in front of her. Suddenly, she jerked her arms up and bit his hand so deep he yelled and let go.

Then she turned and slammed her fist in his eye. He thrust her aside, and she fell to the ground.

Leo fired at Bronco, who fired back.

Leo's bullet whistled by Bronco's ear, but Bronco's bullet slammed into Leo's forehead. Stunned, Leo crashed backward and dropped crazily to the ground, then rolled against the rocks in a heap.

Charity was frantic, getting to one knee and staring at the dead man. She looked up as Bronco came toward her, and she scrambled to her feet, hurrying to fall into his arms. "Oh, Bronco, am I glad to see you."

"Come on, let's get down to Curly," Bronco said.

She had reddening bruises on her chin and left cheek, and she was still shaking, but she was clinging to his vest with her fingers, her face against his chest.

"You've saved me again, Bronco."

"Bronco Jim Hodges."

She stiffened in his embrace, lips tight.

He told her about finding the Sladeks trying to hang Wiley Haines and how he had killed them. "Me and Curly, we hid out from then on."

She caught her breath. "Curly is Wiley Haines?"

"Yeah. He'll tell you all about it."

She drew back in his arms, staring up at him. "I heard Leo and Lucas say that Wiley Haines was my father."

Bronco's face was burning. "Curly wanted to tell you himself. He couldn't care for your mother when she got sick. She died, and Curly had to leave you at the church because the Sladeks wanted him dead."

She pressed her face to his chest and sobbed against him as he continued. He held her a little tighter as he told her Curly's story and how Frank had been in love with Curly's wife.

"Frank wanted to be a father to you."

"He tried," she said, sniffing. "Now he's dead."

"Frank's alive. We had a long talk with him,

Curly and me. Things are kinda straightened out."

She drew back in his arms, tears trickling down her face. "I love Curly. And now you tell me he's my father."

"That's right."

"Hurry. I want to see him."

They mounted and rode down to meet Curly, who was just coming up toward the ridge on foot, leading his horse and the pack mule. He was happy to see them alive, and despite his missing beard, he was still Curly to her. Bronco and Charity reined up, their horses sliding in the dirt.

She dismounted, smiling at Curly. "It's all right now."

"Yeah, it sure is," Curly said.

"Father."

Curly was shaken. "You know?"

She moved close to him, her hands on his arms, and then she moved into his embrace, hugging him tight as he kissed her cheek. They were both crying. She drew back, and he kept staring at her.

"I love you, Curly. Now I understand why."

Curly swallowed, but he couldn't get rid of the lump in his throat nor the flow of tears. "I always loved you, honey. I just couldn't take care of you when they was huntin' me for no reason."

"I know. Bronco told me."

They returned to bury Leo, and that night they camped on the trail; Curly fussed over Charity while she fussed over him.

To get her attention, Bronco told her about Elva and Emmy Lou.

"Oh, my gosh," Charity said.

"What will you do now?" Bronco asked her.

"I'm going to stay with Freddie for a while, until Curly and I can build a house. But I don't want you to go away, Bronco."

"You don't have to worry about that. I'll be camped on your doorstep."

Curly grunted. "Maybe you will, and maybe you won't."

Charity giggled, and the men laughed.

In the morning, they joined up with Krinkle and a day later they turned the horses back to the ranch, where some of the hands had returned. Krinkle stayed to run the place.

Nearing town two days later, the three were enjoying the fresh spring air and sweeping green of the land. Curly and Charity hugged each other a lot. She had dark bruises on her face, but she looked lovelier than ever.

The country was gorgeous. They had seen mule deer darting through the trees. Overhead, a black-billed magpie swept through the clear blue of the sky.

Bronco was feeling pretty good about himself. The past was resolved. He had a badge, there was a pretty girl who was always smiling at him like she might be interested, and he had a good friend. Even better, he had ridden Trigger Foot. He swelled up just a little, and his hat felt tighter. After all, he was a *legend.*

He stretched in the saddle, a smile on his face.

Suddenly, his buckskin shot straight up like a bullet, head down, rump in the air, followed by a sudden spin and leap, then a sudden, brutal stop.

Bronco, taken by surprise, went sailing through the air like a bird right over his horse's head, but he was grabbing air and bouncing around until he hit the dirt with a loud thud. He lay on his back, out of breath.

His buckskin came wandering over and nosed him, then picked up Bronco's hat in its teeth. Bronco jerked it free and growled.

"Yeah, you got even all right. I get the idea."

Hurting some, Bronco sat up, taking the reins.

Charity came riding over in a hurry."Are you all right, Bronco?"

"Now do you believe me?"

She stared down at him and at his buckskin, and she burst out laughing. Curly was grinning as usual.

Bronco got back astride, and his horse was as gentle as a kitten. "You make ole Trigger Foot look like a puppy dog."

In town, they found that Elva and Emmy Lou had moved into the rooming house, but it was Mrs. Bromley who had been nursing Frank Sladek.

He was in a room on the first floor, lying on a couch but fully dressed. Only Mrs. Bromley was there, and Frank was trying to hold her hand, making her fuss at him.

Charity hurried to his side and knelt. "Uncle Frank, are you all right?"

"He's nothing but trouble."

"I'm tryin' to wed this woman."

Mrs. Bromley blushed. "When it's good and legal."

"It's legal," Curly said. "He's a free man."

Frank looked up. "Where are my boys?"

"Dead," Bronco said. "They gave me no choice."

Frank was grim. "Leave me and Charity alone."

Curly hesitated, but he and the others left the room. Charity held Frank's hand and told him she knew about Curly. She related how Leo abducted her and how he had treated her. And how Bronco had tried to arrest Lucas and Leo before his sons had started a fight. Frank fought his tears.

"Now I've lost all my sons. And you."

"I'll always love you, Uncle Frank." She leaned over and kissed his grizzled face.

It was then that Curly burst into the room, frantic.

"Listen here, Sladek, Charity don't belong to you no more."

She stood up with a smile. "It's all right, Curly. I told him. But he's done right by me. Remember I said how he beat Leo for mauling me."

"Well, he can't be all that bad, I reckon."

"What about Freddie?" she asked.

Freddie was in the doorway, arms folded. "Yes, what about me, Frank?"

"Well, yeah, about you, Freddie. You're a

dreadful woman, and afore Charity even got here, I got a letter from Nora, sayin' how you used my money for the ranch and taught her yourself, and I thought, now that's a right smart woman, and I threw the letter away."

Freddie stared at him. "Well, I'll be."

Elva thrust herself into the doorway, pushing Freddie aside. Elva's hands were cuffed behind her back, and her face was pink. "Frank, darling, you have to do something. This awful man is arresting me and my little girl."

Frank chuckled. "Too bad I got away, huh, Esther?"

Elva turned crimson with fury and sputtered, and Bronco drew her back outside. Curly went to help him march the women to the jail, and Bronco sat down to write a letter to Norton to come get them.

The lawmen had supper that night at Mrs. Bromley's with Sally, Freddie, a weary Frank, and Charity. Curly talked about the preacher in town being right handy for him and Freddie, and Frank revealed plans to wed Mrs. Bromley and adopt her daughter, and try to turn his life around.

Bronco went outside alone on the porch, staring at the stars and thinking sadly of his father, but he regretted having killed Frank's sons because although the man himself had gone too far, there was some good in Frank Sladek.

He thought of Charity, trying to figure when the heck it was he fell in love with her. Abruptly the door opened, and Frank came outside, finding his way to the bench and sitting down. Bronco leaned on the post and turned. "I'm sorry about your sons."

"If it hadn't been you, it would have been someone else. It was me what sired 'em, and a lot of the blame is mine, but now I'm bound to set things right. I'm payin' Curly for the land I stole. And I'm deedin' some land and five hundred head in your name to get you started on your own place, whether or not you keep that badge."

"No, thanks."

"In Rad's name then."

Bronco straightened and turned to look at the sincere, anxious look on the man's face. "All right."

The two men shook hands, and it was a strange feeling for both of them. Frank cleared his throat. "Good. Now me and Curly want you and Charity to get married, so I'll send her out here."

"When are you gonna stop telling folks what to do?"

"Ain't you in love with her?"

"Seems like. But she don't know it."

"Women always know, but you got to speak up, Jimmy."

Frank went inside and Charity came out, closing the door behind her. She leaned on the other post and smiled as she drew her shawl about her.

"You're really something," she said. "An outlaw who never was one. A gunfighter. And fistfighter. The only man to ride Trigger Foot. And now you're wearing a badge."

"What about you? Ridin' and shootin' like a man."

"Maybe you can't handle me."

"Never said I wanted to."

"But you want to marry me, Bronco Jimmy Hodges."

"How do you know that?"

"The first time we met, you near fell out of your boots with joy. You've been in love with me ever since. And I felt the same, foolish girl that I am."

"You're loco."

"Am I? See if you can kiss me just once and

stop."

"That's easy."

"If you kiss me more than once, you got to marry me."

"I'll take that bet."

She moved from the post and drew near, her fingers sliding up his leather vest. He gazed down at her lovely face, and he swallowed as his arms slowly encircled her.

She stood on her tiptoes, and he bent his head.

When their lips met, he felt shivers running down his back, all the way to his boots. He hugged her tight, tasting the sweetness, kissing her and kissing her and kissing her, unable to stop until she drew back in his arms.

"I was right," she said, breathless.

Curly came out to separate them, ordering her back in the house, and she paused in the doorway.

"Anything you say, Father. But I want a big wedding."

Curly grinned, and she went back inside.

The two men stood on the porch, considering the way their lives were heading. Bronco grinned to himself as he realized he was going to be Curly's son-in-law. Curly ran his hand over his smooth chin and chuckled.

"You know, Bronco, when we come up the Bozeman, all we were tryin' to do was stay alive. Then everything started spinnin' around and shovin' us every which way until we didn't know what was comin' next. Now look at us."

"Yeah. We fell right back in the quicksand."

ABOUT THE AUTHOR

Western novelist and screenwriter **Lee Martin** grew up on cattle ranches in Northern California. Martin began writing in the third grade and, later in life, wrote and sold 43 short stories before turning to novels with 23 now published. Martin is also a prolific writer of screenplays, mostly Westerns.

Martin's recent novels, *The Grant Conspiracy*, *The Last Wild Ride*, and *Fury at Cross Creek*, all received rave reviews from *True West Magazine* and were based on Martin's screenplays, as is *Fast Ride to Boot Hill*. *In Mysterious Ways*, Martin's new modern suspense Western, received great critical acclaim from *Kirkus Reviews* and *Midwest Book Reviews*. *Trail of the Fast Gun* is the first book of seven in The Darringer Brothers series, all of which have been reissued in paperback and ebook by Vaca Mountain Press, along with many of Martin's earlier novels.

Martin left the practice of law to write full-time, primarily concentrating on Western screenplays and novels, and often converting one to the other. Martin's screenplay for *Shadow on the Mesa*, starring Kevin Sorbo, Wes Brown, and Gail O'Grady, was based on Martin's novel of the same title (Five Star Publishing, 2014). The movie was the second-highest-rated and second-most-watched original movie in Hallmark Movie Channel's history when it premiered in 2013. The film also won the prestigious Wrangler Award given by the National Cowboy & Heritage Museum in Oklahoma City for Best Original TV Western Movie. Several of Martin's screenplays are currently under option by producers. *The Siege at Rhyker's Station* and *The Desperate Riders*, based on two of Martin's screenplays, are both being filmed in the Fall of 2020, and will eventually be available as novels. To learn more, visit Lee Martin Westerns on Facebook.

www.ingramcontent.com/pod-product-compliance
Lightning Source LLC
Chambersburg PA
CBHW031228260626
47169CB00007B/2201